Angels on
Sunset Boulevard

ALSO BY MELISSA DE LA CRUZ

Melissa de la Cruz

Angels on Sunset Boulevard

SIMON AND SCHUSTER

First published in Great Britain in 2008 by
Simon & Schuster UK Ltd
Africa House, 64–78 Kingsway, London WC2B 6AH
A CBS COMPANY

www.simonsays.co.uk

Originally published in 2007 by
Simon & Schuster Children's Books,
An imprint of Simon & Schuster
Children's Publishing Division, New York

Copyright © 2007 by Melissa de la Cruz
Book design by Steve Kennedy
Character illustrations by Sigmund Torre

A CIP catalogue record for this book is
available from the British Library.

ISBN: 978-1-8473-8133-0

1 3 5 7 9 10 8 6 4 2

Printed and bound in Great Britain by
Cox & Wyman, Reading, Berkshire

For my sister, Christina Green, who always loved L.A.
and
for my husband, Mike Johnston, always

After

SATURDAY NIGHT AT THE IN-N-OUT AND A STEADY
parade of drunken rockers, skater kids, Chicano families, frat boys, Beverly Hills princesses, East L.A. gangbangers, Hollywood hippies, artists, and stoners walked through the swinging glass doors, a microcosm of Los Angeles itself.

Nick Huntington sat alone in the front booth, listlessly watching the local citizenry and unconsciously eavesdropping on two hyperactive film types—boneheads, in his humble opinion—honing a movie pitch at the next table, dreams of Hollywood the backbone of every conversation within a ten-mile radius of the studios.

He was holding a fry in midair when he spotted the boy. Nick froze, and the fry dangled on his mouth, the ketchup dripping from the tip and burning the edge of his tongue.

The boy was shaking visibly, his entire body vibrating from an uncontrollable compulsion—knees knocking against each other, teeth chattering, head twitching from side to side. His long hair was matted against his forehead and the back of his neck, and his jeans were torn and holey. After midnight at the In-N-Out Burger on the corner of Orange Drive and Sunset Boulevard and no one paid much attention as he shuffled up to the front of the line, dirt-black fingers trembling as they dug into his pants pockets for grimy dollar bills and change.

"The number one," he mumbled, so softly that the cashier had to repeat it. A flat chemical scent emanated from his pores as if he were sweating aluminum.

"Number one?" she asked again helpfully, breathing through her mouth so she wouldn't smell him but trying not to show it—they got all kinds there.

The boy nodded. His hair was so dirty it looked brown, except for the roots, which were startlingly, shockingly silver, like a halo. He was so skinny his wrist bones protruded from his skin, poking out painfully. His skin was sallow, a drained, sickly, yellow color—junkie yellow—but otherwise it was clear, free of the acne scars and hollowed craters that typically accompanied a drug-induced complexion. He

Melissa de la Cruz

scratched at his three-day-old stubble, then picked at a cuticle on his thumb, watching as the cashier punched in his order.

He accepted his food and turned to look for a seat.

His eyes met Nick's, and a chill went down Nick's spine. It was like looking into the eyes of a ghost. Nick became conscious that his jaw was hanging open and made a deliberate effort to close it. He never did eat that french fry. He'd lost his appetite.

"Aren't you Johnny Silver?" he finally asked.

Nick couldn't believe it. Johnny Silver was supposed to be onstage at the Hollywood Bowl at that very moment, in a comeback concert that was already being heralded as the most important music event of the year—if not the decade, if not the century.

Yet there he was, standing right in front of him. Johnny Silver, his violet eyes boring into Nick's skull, that otherworldly masculine beauty—like David Bowie during his Ziggy Stardust phase—haughty and feral. Dirty and delirious, but alive. The famous Johnny Silver, the boy who would rock the world, standing underneath the fluorescent lights of a fast-food restaurant, looking as if the universe had just run him over.

For the longest time Johnny simply stood there. His eyes glazed, then focused. Tears sprung to his eyes, and they coursed silently down his cheeks, a river of white against the grime.

Nick stood up and approached him cautiously, as a lion tamer would approach his lion. "Johnny, man, what the hell happened to you?"

"I . . . I don't know," Johnny replied, and the shaking intensified. He looked around the fast-food restaurant as if he had no idea how he'd gotten there. "I don't remember anything, except that moment when I came out and strummed my guitar, and I looked out at the audience, at the lights . . . so many people—they'd all come to see me—roaring my name. I blinked, then in a flash everything was gone—the club, the band, the stage, the hotels, Sunset Strip, palm trees, cars, everything disappeared. And I woke up, alone in the desert, as if none of this"—he waved his hand to indicate the whole place and everything beyond it—"had ever existed."

Melissa de la Cruz

A Star Is Born

> "Here we are now going to the Westside,
> weapons in hand as we go for a ride."
> —MOBY (WITH GWEN STEFANI), "SOUTH SIDE"

welcome to
TAP.COM

TAPPED IN....

Your news.
Your space.
Your funeral.
Put up
your stuff,
your videos,
your pics,
your photos,
your music.
Whateva
you gots for
us, we're
into it.

MEMBERSHIP IS FREE.
RESPECT IS NOT.

Member Login:

SCREEN NAME☆

PASSWORD☆

★
search TAP

TajMahal22

TajMahal22 is in your TAP network!

Tapped in: 2005
Female
99 years old
Single/Straight
Hollywood

About me:
Break Staff DJ.
Skaters rule. The
MiSTakes, ArtForum,
AltMusic

View my wish lists:
None
"is this me? love and loyalty"
TajMahal22's blog
Last Login: 4:11 AM

**TajMahal22 has
436 TAP friends**

View my pics/videos:
-half-pipe/Venice/pool-
DOWNLOAD NOW!
-JohnnyandMeForever
CLICK NOW!

COMMENTS

DV844: homeslice is one hot girl! Taj the mastermind
. . . good luck tomorrow!

RickDeckard45: never forget the little people.

JohnnyS11: you asked me to leave you a comment.
here it is. COMMENT

★   [Click to Search for Friends] [Hot New People] [TAPPED IN Archives]   ★

FROM ABOVE THEY LOOKED EXACTLY LIKE A MASS OF buzzing locusts, swelling in a faceless, amorphous, intolerable hunger, growing louder and larger every minute. Taj continued to peek out of the curtains of the topmost penthouse of the Chateau Marmont to get a better look. She bit the top of her thumb anxiously. This was totally out of control. They were chanting his name. Screaming it, even.

"Johnny! Johnny! Johnny!

"Johnny! Johnny! Johnny!

"Johnny! Johnny! Johnny!"

There must have been hundreds of them—maybe even thousands. Taj wasn't sure. Some were holding up signs. JOHNNY SILVER IS MY IDOL!!! WE LOVE YOU JOHNNY!!! WILL YOU MARRY ME JOHNNY?? JOHNNY SILVER ROCKS!!!!!

Waving bouquets of white lilies. (His favorite flower, according to his TAP profile.) Pointing their cell-phone cameras to the sky. Crying into their glitter press-on Johnny Silver T-shirts.

She noticed that traffic on Sunset Boulevard was backed up in all directions, and there were even policemen on horseback trying to manage the crowd. It was absolute mayhem, madness, totally insane. This was the Beatles landing in New York, this was Michael Jackson dangling Prince Michael III off the balcony in Berlin, this was Gwen Stefani in the middle of Tokyo.

Taj pulled the curtains firmly shut, and her tiny gesture sent a ripple through the crowd down below—the roar intensified. She raked a hand through her long, blunt-cut bob of shiny black hair. The severe cut could have been disastrous, but it only served to highlight the exquisite proportions of her beautiful face: large, slightly slanted green eyes, an adorable button nose, that sharp, Keira Knightley chin. She was model-slim and stunning in her striped French sailor's top layered underneath a shrunken antique denim jacket, tight cutoff leggings, and incongruous red patent Doc Martens. Taj didn't dress like anyone else in Los Angeles, where the female population tended toward midriff-baring sweats or plunging jersey V-neck tops. Instead she always looked like she'd stepped out of a funky avant-garde European photo shoot. Edie Sedgwick for a new generation.

She stepped away from the window and took a deep breath. She was not prepared for this. She was not prepared for any of it.

For a moment Taj wondered if it was all a dream. The lavish penthouse suite, the screaming fans, the *Rolling Stone* cover shoot that was underway in the next room.

Tonight Johnny was headlining at the Viper Room, to launch his new album. It was meant to be a small, intimate concert, VIPs and industry insiders only, but demand was so intense, they opened it up to the public. When tickets went at record-breaking levels—two and then four more dates were added. Now his label was talking world tour, even before he had sold one copy. Stadiums in Germany, airfields in France, the Staples Center. They were talking laser light shows, digital projection screens, adding a twenty-piece string orchestra and a gospel choir. It was going to be a production, an event, bigger than Woodstock, bigger than Lollapalooza, bigger than anything the world had ever seen.

And it had all started on TAP.

With a simple TAP request.

JohnnyS11 wants to be your friend. Approve? Deny?

Taj had checked out his page—noted the moody, black-and-white photo of Johnny bent over a guitar, his white-blond bangs covering half his face. Made a note of his interests: taxidermy, ukelele, the Church of the Sub-Genius. Usually Taj never approved requests from boys she didn't know. So many of them were simply collectors, posting up pictures of half-naked women on their sites like baseball cards. The collectors always wanted to know if she had a webcam (she didn't). Her TAP icon was like a magnet for the crazies and the weirdos. But JohnnyS11's friend list was a normal array of slacker boys and nerdy-chic girls. His quote was the usual Andy Warhol one about fame, except in reverse: "In fifteen minutes, everybody will be famous." Taj was intrigued. She'd clicked Approve.

A few days later there was an e-mail message.

Check out my new show. Johnny Silver's Manic Hour.

It was on a college radio station Taj sometimes listened to late at night. Most of the time it was utter crap—just a bunch of pretentious college kids playing their jazz records and thinking they were cool. The kind of kids who turned up their noses at Franz Ferdinand when the band hit the mainstream.

Johnny had started out as a break-staff DJ, one of the high school kids who ran the radio station over the summer and holidays when the college kids went home for break. Johnny's show was different. It was obvious he loved music, and not just what was obscure or hard to find; he was as liable to play a Dylan classic as he was an unknown garage band. His energy was infectious and his playlist eclectic.

On a whim Taj had called the station to request a song, and soon the two of them were talking well into the night, Johnny's voice low and slow over the wires—he had such a radio voice, the kind that melted in your ear and made you want to never turn off the dial. And unlike most DJs, he actually looked like he sounded—sexy. Justin Timberlake might have brought sexy back, but Johnny Silver had never lost it.

That was a year ago. Now Johnny wasn't just playing the records. He was making them. And those songs—those songs he had played for her in her bedroom, those songs he'd sworn were hers alone— had made him a star. It had all happened so fast: He'd posted a few of them on his TAP page, and before you knew it, the kids were downloading them, trading them, begging for more. Then the TAP parties happened. He'd played a beach house in Malibu, a birthday party for some celebrity at Hyde, then to a standing-room-only crowd in Palm Springs. More and more kids began coming to the gigs, and the legend of Johnny Silver grew . . .

And now here he was, at the top of the Chateau Marmont, the famed Hollywood hotel known for the numerous celebrity scandals it had weathered inside its fortresslike walls. John Belushi overdosed in Bungalow 2. Jim Morrison hurt his back jumping off the balcony. Greta Garbo repaired to its premises when she "vanted to be alone."

The penthouse had been Johnny's de facto address for the past several months now. They had become regulars at the pool, grown accustomed to the sight of Sting playing the piano in the lounge or a glimpse of the celebrity couple du jour in the paneled dining room. Taj was half appalled and half amused by the whole thing. Not too long ago she and Johnny had made do with standing in line on La Brea for a cheap Pink's hot dog. Now caviar was being sent to his room by the bucketload.

She walked over to the next room, where a large white seamless background screen had been set up and a large silver umbrella kept the lighting at the optimum angle.

Johnny was sitting on a stool, his guitar on his lap, while the photographer—one of the most famous ones in the business; Taj recognized him from his *Vanity Fair* contributor profile and numerous appearances on VH1's lifestyle shows—was behind the camera, clicking away.

The reporter girl, one of those women who were thirty-five going on fifteen—"ironic" butterfly barrettes in her hair, obligatory Marc Jacobs jacket, clodhopper boots, the zippy personality of a seasoned celebrity ass-kisser—stood to the side, cooing over each shot.

She turned to Taj. "Doesn't he look sooo hot?" Taj shrugged in reply, and the reporter looked nervous. Taj noticed that women who wanted to look like teenagers always seemed to be intimidated when they were in the company of real teenagers. The ersatz meeting the authentic and it wasn't pretty.

"Great shoes!" the reporter said as a friendly gesture, pointing down at Taj's feet. "Where'd you get them?"

"Oh," Taj said, trying to remember. She was a superb bargain-hunter and found most of her treasures in flea markets and designer clearance bins. She also made a lot of her clothing herself, or ripped up vintage items and refashioned them to her own tastes. "Some secondhand store in Pasadena, I think?"

Johnny looked up, moved his bowl-cut bangs off his face, and noticed Taj.

"Where are you going?"

"Out." She shrugged. "My uncle's worried. I haven't been home in a week. Wants to make sure I'm still alive," she joked. Mama Fay was a permissive parent, but even drag queens had their limits. *Come home,* Mama Fay had ordered. *I miss your pretty face.*

He frowned slightly. "Stay."

"Can't."

Johnny sighed, as if she had wounded him deeply.

Once upon a time those limpid violet eyes of his could have induced her to do anything—she had let him *in*, damn it. Had let that voice, and that hair (fine, platinum blond, and soft as a baby duck's feathers), and those eyes do the trick—had let him talk her into doing so many things (like taking off her clothes, like sleeping with him on the first date, like putting up with the other girls—and with Johnny there were always other girls; it was part of the territory, part of the lifestyle, as he liked to call it, and she would have to be "cool" about it if she wanted to be with him, he'd explained).

"I told you, I can't do this anymore." Taj said. "I'm leaving."

Johnny stood up and put his guitar down. "Hold on a sec," he told his entourage.

He followed her to the hallway, grabbed her hands, and stroked them softly, his touch like the tremor of butterfly wings.

"You know it's just a game," he said, smiling. "It's not real."

"It's not that," Taj shrugged. "I just . . . well, you know."

"But I need you, Taj. It doesn't mean anything without you."

Taj sighed. She could never say no to him; that was the problem. "I'll be back. Before the show."

Johnny drew her close and hugged her tightly. He kissed her forehead, her nose, and leaned down to kiss her lips gently, pressing upon her until she closed her eyes and kissed him back. She inhaled his scent—cigarettes and leather and lighter fluid and a trace of something sweet and expensive: cologne that came in crystal bottles from fancy department stores. She had found it in his medicine cabinet one evening and had teased him. It was gone the next day, but the smell remained.

"It's going to be all right," Johnny said, smiling with his eyes half-lidded. "You'll see."

Melissa de la Cruz

"I hope so."

Taj watched him walk—no, strut—back to the photo shoot. The reporter girl was watching them from the doorway.

"Johnny—can we do the interview now? Okay? Tell me, where do you get your inspiration? What made you write 'Bright Eyes'?"

Johnny looked at Taj before answering to see what she would say. Taj remained silent.

"Actually, Haven—it is Haven, isn't it?" Johnny asked, putting an arm around the reporter's shoulders. "I wrote the song for you."

The woman giggled.

Johnny's honeyed voice continued its slow seduction.

Taj rolled her eyes. *Walk out, walk away. You don't have to put up with this anymore. You don't have to be part of this charade.* The whole media maelstrom, the whole star treatment. It was all bullshit. She fetched her skateboard, exited the hotel suite, grabbed the Sunday *Times* from the doorway. She noted another missing-kids headline and while taking the elevator down to the lobby checked to see if she knew anyone they were looking for.

Kids were disappearing all over Los Angeles. It had started a few months back, when a sixteen-year-old Westlake Village girl was reported missing by her parents over Labor Day weekend. She'd never made it home from a beach bonfire. Taj remembered that party. It was a TAP event. The newspaper said that foul play was not suspected at this time; the police suspected the girl had simply run away. Runaways hardly made the news anymore, except that these were private school kids—rich kids with parents who owned summer homes in Malibu. What would they be running away from, exactly? Taj knew there were missing kids from her neighborhood too, but no one seemed to care about kids who disappeared from Echo Park and Hollywood. She folded the paper under her arm and walked out of the elevator to the hotel patio.

It was noon, and the SoCal sun flattened everything in sight, making everything look two-dimensional, as if drawn on a postcard—the guests lounging in bikinis by the David Hockney–blue swimming pool, the pool boys in their crisp white linens. At the Chateau, time seemed to stop in a cocoon of decadent luxury.

She carried her board on her left hip and walked past the valet stand, where a Bentley convertible was parked. Johnny's new car. Another gift from the record label.

Taj lay down her skateboard and pushed off

Melissa de la Cruz

with her back foot—mongo style, they called it, because it was a bit more awkward and harder to pull off—balancing down the hill, cruising all the way. Johnny owned a different set of wheels now, but she still preferred to skate.

The crowd gathered in front of the hotel suddenly went berserk, screaming and hooting. Taj looked up. Johnny had finally come out to the balcony; he was blowing kisses and waving. He caught her eye and smiled, gave her the thumbs-up. Taj nodded but didn't return the smile. She weaved her way through the crying fans.

To them, Johnny Silver was a hero. A rebel. An icon. A god.

But to Taj, he was just the boy she loved who had broken her heart.

welcome to
TAP.COM

HOME
FAVORITES

BROWSE
FORUM

SEARCH
GROUPS

INVITE
EVENT

FILM
VIDEO

MAIL
MUSIC

BLOG
CLASSIFIEDS

TAPPED IN....

Your news.
Your space.
Your funeral.
Put up
your stuff,
your videos,
your pics,
your photos,
your music.
Whateva
you gots for
us, we're
into it.

MEMBERSHIP IS FREE.
RESPECT IS NOT.

Member Login:

SCREEN NAME☆

PASSWORD☆

★
search TAP

NickH3112

**NICKH3112 is in your
TAP network!**
Tapped in: 2006
Male
17 years old
In a relationship
Bel-Air
About me:
Varsity Soccer Captain,
Varsity Crew, Varsity
Tennis, BHCC, NHS

View my wish lists:
None
"uh, am i on the right page?"
NickH3112's blog

Last Login: 3:37 PM
NickH3112 has 469 TAP friends

View my pics/videos:
-Headbutt Goal/
PrivateSchoolLeagueChamps
DOWNLOAD NOW!
-MeandEricBummin
DOWNLOAD NOW!

COMMENTS

MaxitotheMax13: left tix for you at the box office for
tonight. kisses.

MaxitotheMax13: xxooooooxxoooo because I can't stop
thinking about you!

Nick

NICK HUNTINGTON WAS RUNNING LATE. AGAIN. IT was the usual story—too many things to do, too little time to do it all. School, then soccer practice, a shower, dinner with his stepsister, Fish—who at thirteen was left alone way too much, in his opinion, since their parents were never around—trying to get to Sunset before the weekend traffic hit, and failing miserably. He'd been stuck on Santa Monica for what seemed like hours, and when he finally pulled into one of the overpriced parking lots across from the club, the line in front of the Viper Room was ten deep on the sidewalk and snaked all the way down the hill.

"River Phoenix bit it right here," he heard someone say. It was the first thing anyone ever said about the Viper, as if claiming a dead actor added to the

mystique of the place, and it probably did.

Nick wormed his way through to the front. He had VIP tickets, thanks to Maxine; he was supposed to meet her in a booth in the lounge with the rest of the crew. He hoped she wouldn't be too annoyed that he was late again. He really didn't feel up to any Maxine drama right then.

The club was packed wall-to-wall, by far the biggest crowd he'd ever seen at the Viper. *Where did all these people come from?* he wondered. What was the big deal? Sure, he liked Johnny Silver's songs as much as anybody; he'd been one of the lucky few who'd seen the guy play at that party in the desert, when it seemed like everyone attending had experienced the same high, had shared the same visceral energy—it was the first time Nick understood what people meant when they described music as transporting them to a different place. Maybe it had been that TAP thing he'd drunk. That stuff they were handing out to everyone at the event. And afterward he couldn't even remember what was so great about it, only that it had been an experience he wanted to feel again.

What was it about this kid, Johnny Silver? Nick had heard he was some kind of homeschooled music prodigy, some Internet phenom whose popularity had

Melissa de la Cruz

spread from the Los Angeles basin all the way around the world.

Nick walked past the bar and saw Eric McKenzie, his cocaptain and best friend since second grade, sitting in the middle of a leather banquette, leaning over to the adjoining table to chat with Lindsay Lohan's new boyfriend.

"Yo, Nicky, over here!" Eric called. He was a lanky, good-looking boy, with a shock of red hair and a wide forehead. Like Nick, Eric played on all the varsity teams at Bennet Prep. He wasn't the best athlete, but he was certainly the most enthusiastic. Eric was a starter on the varsity soccer team, but he gossiped like a girl—one of his most endearing qualities.

Nick slid into the booth and nodded his greetings to the rest of their party—Clarissa Allen, Maxine's second in command, who had been the most popular girl in school until Maxine had transferred to Bennet Prep. Clarissa was still stung by her dethronement, but she had decided that kowtowing to the enemy was better than being left out of the fun completely. Next to her were several girls who Nick was just start-ing to realize all looked the same, with their fluttery camisoles, tight skinny jeans, and pressed hair. They were as interchangeable as their names: Astley and Ashley and Amory and Avery. Something like that.

And their boyfriends: guys on the soccer team, Trent and Hoyt and Carter and Hilson. His friends. Cookie-cutter versions of the same clean-cut American jock, West Coast version.

He was beginning to wonder how many of his so-called friends he would be able to pick out of a lineup. It wasn't that he didn't pay attention; it was just that part of him was a little sick of his whole scene. They'd all been friends since preschool because their fathers worked with their mothers at the studios, or ran the studios, or starred in the pictures. Some of them already had their own reality TV shows on MTV or A&E; some of them had bit parts on Darren Starr melodramas; all of them thought they were *definitely* going to be famous one day. Just like Nicole Richie, who was just like them, except a little older and a whole lot thinner.

And now they had all gathered here to anoint the newest star on Hollywood Boulevard: Johnny Silver, whose rise to the top had taken them all by surprise. A homegrown, grassroots phenomenon, some kid from the Valley, for God's sake, who had no connections and no money, but who had captured the imagination of the world by talent alone. It was almost so old-fashioned none of them would believe it unless they had seen it for themselves.

Melissa de la Cruz

"Where's Maxi?" he asked Eric.

Eric shrugged. He had a nickname for Maxine too: Radioactive. But he held his tongue. "No idea. She was here a minute ago." Eric handed him a bottle of vodka and an empty glass full of ice. "Drink up."

"Nah, I've got work to do later," Nick said. "Plus I gotta drive."

"Never stopped you before, man." Eric laughed.

Nick smiled. He looked around the room. The show was already two and a half hours late; even for a rock show, this was pushing it. He decided to look for Maxine instead of waiting around. She was probably backstage, since her dad was part owner of the club, and Maxine liked nothing more than to be at the center of the action.

"Excuse me, excuse me," he said, trying not to shove people out of his way.

Nick was surprised to find such a variety of kids at the show—sure, the Beverly Hills posse was represented in the VIP lounge, but the kids in the standing-room areas were a hodgepodge of styles and social classes. Grunge-rockers in their thrift-store plaid; goth girls showing off tongue rings; Mohawks and skinheads and Silver Lake kids with Bettie Page haircuts and boyfriends wearing old bowling shirts and baggy jeans. Artsy Japanese kids with their graffiti sneakers and blinged-out hip-hop kids with their crunk gold teeth and Louis Vuitton. Gorgeous Mexican girls from the barrio in tight tube tops and low-rise jeans that showed off their flat stomachs and J.Lo booty. Then there were the hard core Johnny Silver fans from the suburbs, already in their concert tees, their iPod recorders at the ready—you could tell the kids from the wrong side of the hills by their wide-eyed appreciation of it all.

He cut through the line at the bar—"Watch it!" "Sorry"—and didn't notice the admiring glances many girls threw his way. Nick was seventeen and classically handsome in the movie-star sense: a hint of Brad Pitt along the jawline, soft brown eyes like Orlando Bloom's, a grimace like Josh Hartnett's. He was six-four and moved with an ease that echoed his prowess on the playing fields.

He was the kind of guy who could have anything he wanted. He usually did. Right now he wanted to see his girlfriend.

The goon guarding the backstage door stopped him before he could get any farther.

Nick held up the VIP ticket.

"No dice. Need a backstage pass, dude."

"My girlfriend's back there," Nick protested.

"Yeah, yours and everyone else's." The guard laughed.

"C'mon, man, her dad owns this place. Maxine Ularte."

"You Maxine's boyfriend?"

"Yeah."

"Huh," the guard said.

A group of girls wearing passes that dipped low into their cleavage waved to the guard, and he let them through. Nick craned his neck to see if he could spot Maxine anywhere when the door was opened.

He could see several groupies huddled together, whispering to one another, band members walking around, torsos pale and bare above leather jeans, caterers bringing out more champagne, and yes, a familiar dark head in the mix.

Her back was turned to him, but he could recognize that back anywhere. Maxine's black hair fell silkily down her shoulders; her tanned back was completely bare except for a string that held her halter top together underneath her shoulder blades.

Maxine Ularte—even her last name was sexy. The girl all the guys at school were crazy for, and she had wanted him, had picked him above everyone else.

But then again, that's sort of the way of his world. Ever since he was little, he'd noticed how easy it was to get people to like him. Ever since he could remember, he'd always been the guy. Class president.

National Honor Society. Captain of the soccer team. Everything came easy to Nick—he was rich, good-looking, popular. Although to his credit he never thought of it that way. He was just living his life.

He was going to call her name when he realized she wasn't alone. No, she was straddling someone. Someone whose hands were now all over Maxine's back and undoing the knot that kept her top on. Maxine squirming in some guy's lap. The guy getting up, Maxine still stuck to him like a leech, her legs now wrapped around his waist, her long hair obscuring the guy's face. Not that Nick was too concerned about the guy's face right now; it was his hands he was worried about. One of them had definitely disappeared up Maxine's braless top.

Then the door closed in his face, and he lost sight of the view.

"Hey, wait a minute," Nick argued as he tried to shove his way forward to see if he could still catch them, before they . . . before what? It looked like it was too late to stop whatever it was that needed stopping. Maxine would do what she wanted to do. She was that kind of girl. Uncontrollable. It was part of her appeal.

His stomach did a Montezuma's Revenge—his favorite roller coaster at Knott's Berry Farm when he was a kid. The one that turned you completely upside down.

"Back off!" the guard barked, prodding him with a fat finger to the chest.

He stepped away from the door—wanting to punch the guard, who was smirking in his face—when the back of his legs collided with something.

"Oh, excuse me," a voice behind him said.

"My bad," Nick said, turning to see whose foot he had crushed.

It was a girl, he saw, in his heartbroken haze. A pretty girl with jet-black hair which fell in a graceful swoop above her shoulders. She was looking at him with catlike green eyes. She was gorgeous, even behind the thick square plastic frames she was wearing. An angel shrouded in black, from her leather jacket to her skinny jeans. He'd seen her before—but where?

"Sorry," Nick said again.

"No worries." She smiled.

When had that become such a popular phrase? Nick knew one Aussie kid at Bennet who said it all the time, but now it seemed everyone said it. It usually bothered him, that slack-casual phrase—but from her it didn't. She had sounded genuine, not affected and dismissive.

She held up a backstage pass to the guard and walked easily into the room, leaving Nick alone on the other side of the door, suddenly feeling abandoned by the world.

Then the houselights dimmed. The crowd started their rhythmic clapping. "Johnny. Johnny. Johnny. Johnny." The curtain parted. The show was about to start.

Nick walked blindly back to his seat, groping his way forward in the dark. He did a double take when he arrived at the table.

Maxine was sitting in the booth. She waved at him with her long fingernails. There was no way she could have made her way back to the table before him, was there? Which meant that wasn't Maxine he'd seen backstage . . . that was someone else.

With a sigh of relief, he slid back into the banquette.

"Hey baby, where'd you go?" she purred.

"Looking for you," he said.

"Silly boy. I was here all along."

SHE'D SEEN THAT BOY BEFORE, SHE THOUGHT. THE
dark-haired one who'd bumped into her. It was hard
to forget his face; he was that handsome. Not that Taj
was interested—he had Westside written all over
him, from his black Lacoste shirt to the dark denim
jeans and the Tevas. Just another asshole rich kid,
although he had seemed polite enough, and sorry
that he had stepped on her toe. Ow. She bet he drove
a European car, went to some fancy private school,
and thought the city of Los Angeles ended at La
Cienega—the boulevard of demarcation that no one
from Beverly Hills ever dared to cross. Forget him.

Taj scissored through the maze of bodies pressed
against one another backstage. The excitement in the
air was so strong it was almost a physical sensation—

so many people determined to be part of it, the crowning of a new rock icon. This would be the kind of concert that generations would lie about forever—"I was there the night Johnny rocked the Viper" equal to having been at the Sex Pistols' first gig at Central Saint Martins or having caught Jimi Hendrix at the Monterey Pop Festival.

She'd counted thirteen camera crews set up around the stage; a fifty-foot boom hovered above the floodlights. If rock history was going to be written tonight, *Access Hollywood* wasn't going to miss any of it. The show was even going to be projected on giant video screens on Sunset Boulevard to the throng of adoring fans who hadn't been able to get tickets.

"Pizza?" one of the stagehands offered, motioning to the crafts table.

"Sure, why not." Taj nodded, taking a slice. It was piping hot, and she almost burned the roof of her mouth when she took a bite. "Wow. This is good. Where's it from?"

"Brooklyn."

"Joe Peep's in the Valley?"

"No. *Brooklyn*. As in, next to Queens?" the guy replied. "Nothing but the best for Mr. Silver."

Taj almost choked on the slice. Flown in from Old Fulton Street? No way. It was a joke she and Johnny had cooked up when the rep from the label had asked him what he wanted—if he had a list of requirements before the show. Taj had thought up the most outlandish requests she could think of—perfume to be pumped in the air vents in the newly remodeled toilets, silver M&M'S only—and as a joke had written "Pizza from Grimaldi's," the famous New York City shop that she'd visited the one time she was in the city for band camp.

Neither of them had really believed they would get any of it. And yet weren't there heaping crystal bowls filled with silver M&M'S everywhere? And Taj would bet that if she visited the bathroom she would be doused in Route du Thé perfume and the porcelain seat would be brand-new. It struck her then that this was truly happening, that it wasn't a joke anymore, wasn't a prank that they had pulled on the world.

Johnny was really going to be a star—he already was a star—the kind of star that spoke for a generation, with music that touched cheerleaders and misfit outcasts alike. Early reviews of the album had compared its genre-shattering appeal to Nirvana's *Nevermind*, to Public Enemy's *Fear of a Black Planet*, to Radiohead's *The Bends*.

Where was he, anyway? Taj knocked on Johnny's door, and hearing no answer turned the knob and stepped inside.

"Oh my God! I'm so sorry!" She backed away from the door, her cheeks crimson. The half-naked couple stirred from the couch. For a panicked heartbeat, Taj had thought it was Johnny, but she could see now that it wasn't. Thank God.

The boy on the couch was Sutton Werner, Johnny's boy-wonder manager. Sutton leaned back, and the girl on his lap, a topless dark-haired beauty, stretched her arms over her head, yawning. Neither seemed particularly bothered by the interruption.

"Looking for Johnny?" Sutton asked, his amber eyes glowing. He was a good-looking guy, except that his eyes were slightly too small, the nose was just slightly too big, and the mouth, a hard line, was almost cruel. Taj, who was an aficionado of eighties teen flicks, thought there was something very James Spader in *Pretty in Pink* about him. Beautiful but repulsive.

Sutton had come into their lives just like any other fan, as a TAP request, and had been one of the first to pick up on the popularity of Johnny's songs. Then he had become more than that—he had arranged the impromptu TAP parties, had been the one to bring the record label on board, had booked the Viper Room, had promised them—Was there still a them? Taj wondered—the world.

"Yeah, you know where he is?"

"Check the bathroom." Sutton said, lazily stroking the girl's hair.

"Thanks."

"And Taj?"

"Yeah?"

"Tell him it's all going to be okay. All right? He knows what to do."

Taj knocked on the bathroom door.

"Come in," a gruff voice replied.

She entered the room. Sure enough she inhaled a massive dose of Barneys-brand perfume.

Johnny looked up from the sink, where he was preparing the solution. "I knew it was you," he said. His bangs were plastered to his forehead, and Taj knew if she touched his face, his skin would be damp. She tried not to look upset, not wanting to get into another argument.

"Johnny, what are you doing?" she asked, crossing her arms in front of her chest.

"Hooking up," he said, tying a rubber cord around his forearm, and tightening it.

"I can see that. You don't need that shit. Who got it for you? Sutton?"

"Baby, you don't even know what I need," Johnny sang softly.

"You don't even know what's in there."

"Whatever it is, it works for me. Are you sure you don't want any?"

"Yeah, I'm sure."

Taj shook her head. TAP—The Angels' Practice. It wasn't just a website. Or more specifically, the website was only the beginning. It was also a movement, a phenomenon, and a drug. Nobody knew what was in the drug, but its effects were astonishing—otherworldly, like taking heroin, ecstasy, and acid all at once. Not only did you feel fantastic, but all your senses shifted, and your mind opened to another plane. It was all-natural, organic; most of the ingredients were sold at Whole Foods, except for that one variable, of course—the angel factor—and no one was sure what it was. Some kind of plant that they were growing down south? Some kind of new hybrid from the rain forest? It didn't matter. All the kids knew was that it made them feel good. The beauty of it was that it wasn't even illegal. It was something in the water; the mixture was what made it potent. But no one was quite sure how.

Best of all there were no consequences. At least none that anybody could see. There was no crash, no afterburn, no need to cut it with alcohol to soften the harsh landing when the high faded. After taking TAP, you were just like you were before, only more peaceful. It wasn't even supposed to be addictive. But tell that to Johnny.

"Good luck tonight," Taj said, watching him sink the needle into his arm and his face relax as TAP hit his bloodstream. He was mainlining now. Most people just drank it—TAP mixed with Kool-Aid was the beverage of choice for most. "I'll be outside, watching."

He nodded dreamily, already lost in his own universe, barely even acknowledging her presence.

Taj found her seat in front of the stage, off to the side. Sutton was already seated in his usual place, where he could survey the stage and the crowd at the same time. He was alone; the girl he had been with was gone. She'd left a mark on his neck, though, an ugly purple hickey that he hadn't bothered to cover up. He offered her a glass of beer. "To Johnny."

"To Johnny," she replied, accepting it.

The chanting of the crowd grew impatient, and the TV reporters gathered behind them were muttering complaints underneath their breath. Taj could hear them talking about their kids, wondering when they would be allowed to go home; the show was going to be too late to make the eleven o'clock news anyway; it would have to be saved for the morning program.

"Can you feel it?" Sutton asked, wagging his eyebrows. "The coming of the supernova?"

"The death of a star?" Taj asked skeptically.

"Technically, yes," Sutton grimaced. "But what happens before a star dies? It goes supernova— releasing an incredible explosion of energy and light into the known universe. An explosion so powerful it resonates throughout the entire galaxy."

Taj grunted. Sutton could be so trig sometimes, what they called cuckoo. But even trigs could be useful. She and Johnny had trusted Sutton, had let him and his ideas into their lives. Taj wondered if that had been wise of them—but it was too late now, wasn't it? It was too late to back out. Too late to pop the genie back into the lamp. Too late to ask for those three wishes back from the traveling monkey.

She sat back and watched the stage. This was everything they had dreamed about, this night, the record sales, the attention of the entire world. This was what Johnny had been working for ever since he was an eight-year-old kid strumming his first Fender Stratocaster with its flamed finish and vintage tube amp.

The houselights dimmed. The curtain parted. Taj leaned forward in her chair, her breath caught in her throat. *Good luck, Johnny* . . .

Johnny Silver stood at the microphone, his guitar in

hand, his shiny platinum hair so bright it dazzled the eyes, his beautiful face solemn as he struck a chord.

"This is for you, Taj," he said gruffly into the mic. He strummed the first chord, and there was an explosion of light, a white light that blinded the audience and shot out from the middle of the stage where Johnny was standing.

The crowd gasped. And clapped and cheered. "Awesome effects, man!" "That was off the chain!" "It looked so . . . *real*!" "Woo-hoo! What a way to start the show!"

Then the smoke cleared.

All that was left was the microphone stand.

Johnny and his guitar were nowhere to be found.

The band stood in shock. They scratched their heads, glancing behind their instruments with puzzled expressions on their faces.

There was a murmur from the crowd. An annoyed grumbling that was threatening to turn into anarchy. They had waited three frigging hours already. The manager came out onto the stage and waved his hands to silence the crowd. "Folks, I'm sure there's an explanation for this. We ask for your patience."

What the hell? What are they playing at? Taj wondered. *What's going on?* Where the fuck was Johnny? Was this part of the act?

Several long minutes ticked by. And finally the manager came back out to the front of the stage and said the words that would change Taj's life forever.

"Johnny's gone. He's disappeared."

The ensuing uproar was enough to cause a riot on Sunset Boulevard, where thousands had gathered on the streets and had witnessed the moment live on the giant video screens. No show. Johnny was gone. He wasn't going to play. Johnny Silver had left the building.

"I told you," Sutton said dreamily as he sipped his drink and chaos erupted all around them as ticket holders demanded their money back and started throwing chairs and tables to the ground.

"Supernova."

Melissa de la Cruz

Disappearance

"Disappear Here"

—BRET EASTON ELLIS, *LESS THAN ZERO*

TAPPED IN....

**Your news.
Your space.
Your funeral.
Put up
your stuff,
your videos,
your pics,
your photos,
your music.
Whateva
you gots for
us, we're
into it.**

**MEMBERSHIP IS FREE.
RESPECT IS NOT.**

Member Login:

SCREEN NAME☆

PASSWORD☆

★
search TAP

**You are logged in as TajMahal. If you are not
TajMahal22 click here:**
View my pics/videos:
[No New Pics/Videos]

TAPPED IN . . . The latest news from your world

8:20 PM **TAP-editguru** writes: *ROCKER STALKER ALERTS!*
Because you begged for it, here are the latest **Johnny
Silver** sightings. This dude is bigger than Elvis! He's
everywhere . . .

razrblade222: SWEAR i saw **Johnny** at Fairfax & Olympic
at the gas station last night. Looked good, like he'd
been working out. Wearing sunglasses. Aviators.

Silvergirl1099: he was just down in Santa Monica near
the pier. i said ni but he ran away . . .

musicismylife2751: writing from Amsterdam, **J.S.** is
playing in a small club down here. Calls himself
Anders King. His hair is BLACK now.

havingablondmoment171: at heathrow, think the guy
across from me is **Johnny**. but he's wearing a cap over
those silver locks. hard to say.

COMMENTS

DV844: just checking in on you. hope you are good. we
miss **Johnny** too.

Formatone101: hang in there **Taj**, he'll be back. We
believe!

RickDeckard95: what div said.

Alternate_future674: **Johnny Silver** will return. Be
strong. be chill.

[99 New Comments] Display?

★ [Click to Search for Friends] [Hot New People] [TAPPED IN Archives] ★

TAJ'S PARENTS WERE MUSICIANS—DAD PLAYED THE
cello, Mom sang opera. They died in a car accident
when Taj was four years old, on the way to a show.
She didn't remember much about them, although
Mama Fay tried her best to fill in the details, recount-
ing stories of her mother's passionate performances
and her father's rigorous practices. When Taj asked
what they were like, Mama Fay responded with stock
answers—that her mother was pretty and smart, her
father dashing and handsome.

But Taj preferred to imagine that her mother was
a diva, demanding and pretentious, waltzing around
making declarations while waving her hands in the
air, and that her father was a lady-killer who'd made
women swoon with his virtuoso cello playing. That

they were a fun, exciting, and dangerous couple, instead of the ordinarily pleasant-looking people in the pictures she had left. It was just too sad otherwise. Missing them was such a huge part of her life she hardly even noticed it anymore.

She'd been raised by her uncle, a drag queen who performed nightly at a cabaret in West Hollywood aptly named Don't Tell Mama! They lived in a small bungalow in the Hollywood Flats, next door to a methadone clinic and across the street from a needle-exchange center. Although that might change soon, as prices were skyrocketing all over L.A., and their ranch house with its chain-link fence and rusty Pinto on blocks in the driveway had heaved itself past the half-million-dollar mark.

Taj stuffed her gear in her backpack and hollered across the room to let Mama Fay know she was leaving.

Mama Fay's stiletto bedroom slippers—pink satin with pom-poms—clacked delicately down the wood floor. Her silk housecoat barely concealed the evening's costume: Lurex short shorts, spangly corset, fishnet thigh-high stockings. "You're off, baby doll?" Mama Fay asked, stirring her martini with her pinkie finger. "All right, be careful, okay? Be home by the time I get up. Else you know I'll worry."

That was the extent of Mama Fay's parenting.

Mama Fay routinely got up by three o'clock in the afternoon, usually with a killer hangover. Taj knew Mama Fay meant well, but the actual raising of a child had been almost comically difficult for her. Taj had survived a peripatetic childhood, dragged around the globe as her uncle chased down cabaret gigs. She was always the kid in school who never had the right supplies, who was always borrowing pens and paper from her classmates, whose parent had forgotten to sign the field-trip release form.

In a way, it had been liberating. After they'd finally settled back in Los Angeles when she was eleven years old, Taj had been allowed to roam the city streets without supervision. She knew every back alley and shortcut and the best place to get Baja fish tacos (on Whittier Boulevard).

"Bye," Taj said, giving her uncle a peck on the stubbly cheek that no amount of foundation could hide. She had to be at the station in an hour, and it was going to take that long to get to the Westside, if she was lucky.

It was a week after Johnny's disappearance at the Viper Room, and she hadn't heard a word from him since then. Not one e-mail, not one text message, not one phone call. Sure, they had been arguing for a long time now about the way everything was going down; Taj wasn't even sure if he still considered her his girlfriend. In the end maybe to him she'd just been one of the many girls who were always around. God forbid he thought of her as a groupie.

Sutton was inscrutable and vowed that he was just as shocked as she was at Johnny's sudden disappearance. Taj didn't know what to think. Maybe Johnny had just wanted to take some time off, to lay low while the hype died down. Except—and that was the weird thing about it—his disappearance only made his fame grow larger, more mythical. If anything, more people were drawn to TAP and his music than ever before. He had the most friends on the site; she wondered who was keeping up his page. Her page was out of control. People were convinced she knew where Johnny was. Johnny's numbers even beat out the Internet centerfold (the most downloaded girl on TAP)!

He hadn't wanted to sell out, that's what the kids were saying. He was too cool for it all. He didn't want to be part of it. Yeah. Johnny Silver was never going to play *Saturday Night Live* or stumble onstage at the Grammys or read cue cards at the fucking MTV Awards. No way. He was an *artist*. The real thing.

The show had been broadcast on loop on the

twenty-four-hour news channels for days. Taj was so sick of watching that white light shine and engulf Johnny. What was that? Some sort of trick. It had to be. The label had decided to release the album anyway, and it had shot to number one immediately, hovering above the real bands as well as the made-up ones whose provenance could be traced to reality shows.

Wherever he was, Taj hoped he was safe.

She made her way from their street to Santa Monica Boulevard. There was an old song from the eighties that went, "Nobody walks in L.A." Taj smiled to herself as she thought, *Nobody rides the bus, either.* She joined her fellow passengers at the stop: elderly couples, Mexican housekeepers, poor teenagers like herself who didn't have parents to provide shiny black Audis on their sixteenth birthdays. A lumbering Metro pulled up to the curb, and Taj followed the dismal procession. She found a seat in the back and settled in for the long journey.

She leaned her head on the windowpane and watched as a speeding BMW suddenly came to an abrupt stop at the light, tapping the fender of the Porsche in front of it. The two cars pulled to the side, and their owners climbed out of their expensive sports cars to check the damage. Just a tap, just a little nick. The two drivers shook their heads, shrugged their shoulders, climbed back inside their cars, and drove away. If she owned a car like that, Taj thought, she would be a lot more careful driving it.

Taj hooked her knees against the seat in front of her and took out her journal, scribbling as the bus ambled past the neon lights of West Hollywood, past the triple-X porno theaters and the twee rainbow flag–waving coffee shops and the brightly lit *Hustler* emporium. She and Johnny had been thrown out of the porno palace once for being underage. They had laughed at the fur handcuffs and the plastic sex toys, snickered at the video of Tommy and Pam that was playing overhead.

She looked out the window. The bus was taking them through Beverly Hills proper, and Taj marveled at how the streets suddenly became much wider—as if the city began to exhale right on the boulevard. She stared at rows and rows of gated mansions hidden behind two-story hedges. Beverly Hills was like a fairy tale, filled with castles and servants and princesses who drove Mercedes-Benz chariots. She smiled at the thought of Johnny joking that once he made it big, they would get the biggest house on the block. And not one of those suburban McMansions on *Cribs* either.

But Taj would never want to live there. What was Beverly Hills anyway but the glorified kingdom of cosmetic dentists and plastic surgeons and retired Republican donors? It was no place for her and Johnny. Not that there was a "her and Johnny" anymore.

Finally the bus deposited her on the outskirts of campus in Westwood. She unhooked the straps that held her board to her backpack, kicked it to the sidewalk, and glided down the stone footpaths toward the music building. The first week of January all the college kids were still on semester break, and the place was blank and desolate, atypically gloomy for Los Angeles.

Taj had taken over Johnny's show. *Johnny Silver's Manic Hour* became so much more popular than the college kid's he was filling in for that he got the gig full-time.

When he'd signed to the label, he hadn't wanted to give up his show. But his popularity took off and who better to take the slot than Johnny's girlfriend? So she'd volunteered to take it over, to keep house while they waited for Johnny to return. The job was easy enough, even though it was a pain to get to.

The college radio station was located in the basement of the music building in three small shabby rooms: an office and two broadcasting studios. There was a ground-level window that attracted the random curious onlooker and a nightly check by the campus police to make sure the kids weren't using the space to hook up or throw parties.

Stacks of CDs were lined up neatly on shelves, and there were several crates of old vinyl records. Two CD players, a turntable, and a computer filled with MP3s were hooked up to the system. The crew at the station was in the middle of transferring all the music to digital files, and soon being a DJ would be just as simple as putting an iTunes list together.

Taj settled into the rickety leather office chair, put on the Bose headphones, clicked on the computer screen, and played Johnny's signature opening: "Hallelujah," by Jeff Buckley. *I heard there was a secret chord that David played and it pleased the Lord . . .*"

As the song came to a warbling close, she whispered into the microphone, "This is Taj Holder in for Johnny Silver. This one is for Johnny, wherever you are . . ."

As usual ever since Johnny had vanished, as soon as she finished, the phone lines lit up and the computer screen began popping with a dozen IM messages.

His fans.

celestialgdess: where he at taj? lighting a candle for johnny ...

dingorider: peace&luv forever...Johnny silver rules!

sadboy22: 7 days and counting...miss u Johnny...

She let the songs play automatically from his list; she knew what they wanted, those kids waiting in the dark for their songs. Johnny's show didn't play at parties up in the Palisades, or for kids cruising Sunset—it was for the ones like Taj was once. Those who were stuck at home with headphones on, trying to drown out the sound of the world, feeling like the only one who understood was a voice on the radio . . .

Taj logged in to TAP and started reading the latest Johnny Silver sightings. The night at the Viper, Taj had been sure it was just some kind of joke—Johnny having a tantrum and refusing to play the biggest show of his career. But it just didn't seem funny anymore.

She'd harassed Sutton, as well as Johnny's publicist and the folks from his record company, but none of them had a clue as to his whereabouts. TAP was full of rumors—Johnny had fled to rehab in South America. Or had joined a monastery in Tibet. Or was living in a commune in Utah, or on a beach in Phuket.

Maybe they were right. Maybe Johnny was out there somewhere surfing his brains out. But Taj didn't think so. More likely Johnny was in some motel room somewhere with that needle in his arm. She hoped, not for the first time and with a sudden panic, that he wasn't dead.

The phone rang. Taj was glad of the reprieve from her morbid thoughts.

"Hey, is this Taj?" a friendly voice inquired.

"This is Taj."

"Hey. Just wanted to see if you could play that song—you know, Johnny's song."

When Johnny's promo CD had arrived, fresh and shiny in its plastic package, she was surprised to find that the first song on the playlist was one he had never played for her before. It was a beautiful song, filled with ache and longing. He had told her it was going on his new album, but he'd never let her hear it while he was working on it. She recognized the first chord—it was the same one he'd played before he'd vanished in a puff of smoke.

Since then, it was the most requested song on the radio. She played it on every show, and it was inevitable that someone would request it at least several times in the night.

"Sure, and who can I say requested it?"

"Nick. Nick Huntington," the caller said, yelling over the sound of traffic in the background.

"Thanks, Nick Nick Huntington."

She queued up the song, abruptly taking off the Stellastarr track that was playing. "This one is for Nick Huntington. Off of Johnny Silver's new album. Enjoy."

The song played, and like clockwork the phone lines lit up like Christmas. But instead of answering, Taj closed her eyes, counting softly, one, two, three, four, as the lines blinked off one by one.

Johnny's song played on her headphones. Taj mouthed the words, the lyrics seared in her brain: *Is this me? Love and loyalty. What do I see?*

Even the IMs stopped popping.

Like her, everyone was just listening . . .

welcome to **TAP.COM**

HOME BROWSE SEARCH INVITE FILM MAIL BLOG
FAVORITES FORUM GROUPS EVENTS VIDEO MUSIC CLASSIFIEDS

TAPPED IN . . . The latest news from your world

TAPPED IN....

Your news.
Your space.
Your funeral.
Put up
your stuff,
your videos,
your pics,
your photos,
your music.
Whateva
you gots for
us, we're
into it.

MEMBERSHIP IS FREE.
RESPECT IS NOT.
☆

Member Login:

SCREEN NAME☆

PASSWORD☆

★
search TAP

10:45 PM **anon** writes: Spotted leaving Beverly Hills in a huff, **NickH3112** with a huge chip on his shoulder. Heard screaming from the pool house (not the good kind). Methinks **Little Miss Maxi** gave him an eyeful (not the good kind).
CLICK HERE to check out what made Nick check out.

[Two comments]
[Add a Comment]

COMMENTS

---

sweetsalmon4115: No Way! No Way! No Way! No Way!

Prettier_than_thou538: about time he found out da truth, donchathink?

★ [Click to Search for Friends] [Hot New People] [TAPPED IN Archives] ★

Nick

NICK HUNG UP HIS CELL PHONE AS THE OPENING chord to Johnny's song filled the Harmon Kardon speakers in his Bentley convertible. He'd never called in to the show before, but after what had happened that night, there was something about the girl's voice on the radio that had spoken to him. That had made him feel less lonely somehow. He drove up to the house and punched the code into the security box that opened the gate. He waited as the electronic control swung the steel door open slowly; the minute he could fit the car past it, he floored the engine, almost scraping the side door, then zoomed up the winding driveway toward the main entrance.

The house was dark, the windows shut, shades and curtains drawn, which was usually a sign that its four occupants were gone for the evening, along with the day staff of two. He unlocked the door and punched in another code to deactivate the burglar alarm. There were so many security codes to remember—one for the gate, one for the house, one for the pool fences—not to mention the proliferation of ATM codes, computer passwords, and various e-mail account access codes, that he kept a piece of paper in his wallet with all of them written down. Not a great idea, he knew, but it was the only way he could keep track instead of getting everything all jumbled in his brain.

He locked the door behind him and entered the kitchen, surprised to see a light shining in the alcove by the stove.

"Oh!"

Slam!

Fish jerked down the screen on her laptop and the halo of light disappeared.

"Everything all right in there?" Nick asked, turning on the switches, flooding the room with fluorescent light.

Fish was sitting cross-legged on a stool, a guilty look on her face. "You scared me!" she said, putting a melodramatic hand up to her head and pretending to faint. Fish never gave up an opportunity to test out

her acting skills; she had been overreacting to everything that happened in her life ever since she was
born. It was one of the many things Nick loved about
his stepsister.

"Whatcha hiding?" Nick asked, walking over so
he could look over her shoulder, although the laptop
was still shut.

"Nothing." Fish shook her head, running her fingers on the top of the computer protectively, although
her tone of voice suggested a wealth of mystery.

"What's wrong, shrimp?" Nick asked affectionately. Fish's real name was Fish—her mother was a
famous environmental activist. She'd married Nick's
father when Fish was just two years old and Nick six.
Fish spent the summers with her dad, a corporate
lawyer in New York. People often remarked how
much Nick and Fish looked alike, and neither of
them ever bothered clarifying the fact that they
weren't blood related. Each was the only sibling the
other would ever have.

"I told you, nothing," Fish said insistently. "Why the
third degree?" she asked, jutting out her chin and
assuming a defiant pose. Now she was playing an
aggrieved, defensive suspect from a film noir. Their
parents had effectively squashed Fish's acting bug;
neither of them approved of the entertainment industry,

even though—or maybe because—Nick's father was a powerful movie producer. They had forbidden Fish from joining the profession, at least until she turned eighteen, so Fish had to make do with school roles and infusing her ordinary life with as much outsize excitement as possible.

"What's up with you?" she asked hesitantly, as she gingerly lifted up the screen and began pecking at the keyboard. Occasionally a pinging sound would indicate the pop-up of a new message.

Nick shrugged and walked over to the Traulsen, the refrigeration unit his stepmother had installed during last year's renovation. It was the same kind that four-star restaurants used to keep their beluga chilled to an icy twenty-eight degrees. The Huntingtons' was mostly used to store twenty different kinds of soda, bottled water, and coffee drinks. He perused the drink selection and took out a Red Bull.

"Are you sure you're okay?" she asked, watching as he closed the fridge door and pulled out a stool across from her by the island alcove.

In answer he pushed open the tab and took a gulp from the silver and blue can. The tart, citrus flavor gave him that instant caffeine high he craved.

"You're not having any Maxi Pad problems?" she asked. Fish glanced up from the screen at her stepbrother occasionally while her fingers flew over the keyboard.

He took a long gulp from the can. "We broke up." That was easier to say than he had thought it would be.

"Yeah, I heard," Fish said softly, her eyes downcast. "It's all over TAP."

"Already?" Nick asked, shocked even though he shouldn't have been. "What does it say?" he asked.

In answer, Fish turned her laptop toward him, and Nick read the item.

"Unbelievable," he breathed. He had confronted Maxine only an hour—no, forty-five minutes ago; already TAP.com—had all the gory details. Nick and Maxine were perennial boldface names in the "Tapped In" column. There was even a link to the picture he'd found on her phone that evening that was obviously not meant for his eyes. How the hell did that get out already? He clicked on the link, and that nauseous feeling returned. It was a picture of Maxine and Sutton Werner in a passionate lip-lock backstage before the Johnny Silver concert at the Viper Room. He recognized the halter top Maxine had been wearing that night.

"If it's any consolation, he's totally *eww*," Fish declared, channeling her best Summer Roberts impersonation.

Nick grimaced. It stung, but then part of it was his fault; he'd heard the rumors—they'd been on TAP for months—that Maxine was stepping out on him with Sutton Werner, but he'd adamantly refused to believe them, dismissing it as idle gossip. Sutton Werner? That loser? The one who wore an ascot to class?

He had been willfully blind. He'd told himself not to trust what he'd seen with his own eyes. Had talked himself into believing that somehow, because she was seated at the table when he got there, she couldn't have been backstage hooking up with some- one else. When for all he knew Maxine had spotted him, too, and had used the shortcuts around the club to fool him. Yeah. That was probably what happened.

He could see that now. Pictures were worth a thousand words, and his girlfriend had been stupid enough to keep one on her phone. But now that he knew the truth, did he really feel any better?

"At least you finally know what she's really like," Fish said, being herself for a change.

Nick sighed, and his right cheek twitched. Why had he let Maxine run all over him like that? He still couldn't figure it out. He'd had girlfriends before, but none of them had ever cheated on him, at least not that he knew about. None of them had ever flaunted their cheating so unapologetically.

His cell phone rang. Maxine.

He rejected the call, sending it straight to voice mail. He would deal with her later.

Fish shut down the computer and raked a hand through her curly blond hair. "Spare me a fifty?" she wheedled.

"What do you need money for?" he asked.

"Sex. Drugs. Rock and roll. The usual." She grinned. "Don't make me depend on the kindness of strangers."

"Seriously," Nick pressed.

"Seriously?" she asked warily, the Blanche DuBois fading from her accent.

"Doesn't Dad give you enough allowance?"

"Are you kidding? Mackenzie Ryan gets like three times what I get. *And* credit cards. Donovan Rainer uses her mom's black AmEx. You think Evelyn is ever going to hand over the plastic? C'mon, it's just a fitty. Please?" For the first time that evening, Fish sounded her age.

"All right," he said as he opened his wallet and handed her a hundred-dollar bill. "Don't spend it all in one place."

"Thanks!" Fish said, pecking him on the cheek. There was a long beep from the front gate, and Fish called up a website on her computer screen that, like every television and computer in the house, was linked to their security camera. It showed a yellow taxicab idling by the curb.

"My ride."

"You're going out?" Nick asked, a trace of surprise in his voice, although he tried to camouflage it to spare her feelings.

"For your information, I'm going to a party," Fish said, as if she went out every weekend. But it was only recently that Fish had finally showed signs of having a social life. Nick had understood she was a little bit of an outcast at school—most of her class- mates didn't know what to make of her melodramatic gestures. But that had all changed a few months ago, when Fish suddenly began bringing friends home. Skinny little girls with glitter on their eyelids who erupted into self-conscious giggles whenever he walked into a room.

"Well, have fun. Does Evelyn know you're out of the house after midnight?"

"Uh, dude, do you see Evelyn here? What Evelyn doesn't know will never hurt her."

Nick shook his head. When he was thirteen there was no way he would have dared sneak out of the house at midnight, but things were different now— Fish came and went as she pleased. She made her own schedule and answered to nobody. And since she was pulling all A's at Tuning Fork, that hippie-dippie art school she attended, their parents practically let her do whatever she wanted—as long as it didn't involve film or TV auditions.

She brushed by Nick, and something on her arm caught his eye. "Hey," he said, catching her wrist and pulling it closer to the light.

"What?" she asked, annoyed.

He looked intently at the green ink that peeked out from underneath her colorful collection of wristbands and thread bracelets. He pushed up on the rubber bands, revealing a tiny tattoo on the inside of her wrist.

"When did you get this?"

"I dunno, coupla weeks ago." Fish shrugged, pushing her wristbands over it again. She wrenched her hand away. "I'm late, dude. See you later."

Nick watched her leave. He'd seen that tattoo before. Johnny Silver famously sported a similar one on the inside of his forearm. He'd seen it somewhere else too—Maxine, the last time they were together, though that seemed ages ago. He was kissing the back of her neck, lifting her shirt from behind when he saw it, tattooed on the small of her back, just above her hips . . .

A pair of angel wings.

TAPPED IN . . . The latest news from your world

TAPPED IN....

Your news.
Your space.
Your funeral.
Put up
your stuff,
your videos,
your pics,
your photos,
your music.
Whateva
you gots for
us, we're
into it.

MEMBERSHIP IS FREE.
RESPECT IS NOT.
☆

Member Login:

SCREEN NAME ☆
[   ]

PASSWORD ☆
[   ]

★
search TAP

9:14 PM **doogie** writes:

Screw New Year's.
Party like it's last year.
Benedict Canyon.
Call/Text 310-555-5555 for deets.
Bring yourself.
Bring a friend.

[Eight comments]
COMMENTS [Add a comment]

---

mystic_sally323: this is THE BASH . . . bring it on or face the music! See you suckers there!

rolandf52: called the number. nothing. what up?

mystic_sally323: try again, it's just overloaded maybe

shazam117: there's no party. it's a joke. get a life people.

Hellothere03: don't forget the word!

provacateur27: yeah, it's tradition by now . . .

lt_girl713: don't you mean a ritual???

kingmaker922: ritual. Haha. Good one.

SOMEONE RAPPED ON THE DOOR OF THE STUDIO. TWO
sharp knocks followed by a pause, then one sharp
knock. Taj grinned. Deck and DV8 had arrived. She
walked over to let them in, and her two best friends
grinned at her from the doorway.

"There she is!" DV8 smiled. Her real name was
Divbie Han, but no one ever called her that. She mostly
went by Div. "How you doing, girl?"

Behind her was Deck, short for Rick Deckard, Kevin
Zoleta's preferred moniker, after the badass cop in
Philip K. Dick's *Do Androids Dream of Electric Sheep?*—
a book he carried in his back pocket for luck—the same
character played by the badass Harrison Ford in *Blade
Runner*, Deck's all-time favorite movie.

Deck was a gangly kid, almost freakishly tall and

thin, all bony knees and elbows, with a razor-cut bowl shag and a prominent Adam's apple. He had one of those Roman faces—haughty and imperial-looking until he smiled. They had been friends since the fourth grade, and they lived in the same neighbor-hood. He had professed his undying love for Taj the unfortunate night of the eighth grade graduation dance, and he had been crushed when Taj had gently turned him down, saying she only saw him as a friend.

They'd met Div at East Hollywood High their freshman year, the year Div's family moved to the United States from Laos. She could hardly speak a word of English then, and everyone at school had brushed her off as a total FOB (Fresh off the Boat) in her high-waisted polyester pants from Marshal's, acrylic sweaters from Wal-Mart, coke-bottle glasses, and awful poodle perm. But after a few months at East Holly and watching nonstop American cable tel-evision, Div had suddenly transformed into one of the hottest chicks in school. She'd lost the accent, cut her hair into a gamine pixie, and learned to wear contacts and shop on Melrose.

Deck and Div were clothed similarly in tight-fit-ting T-shirts that hugged their lanky frames and peg-leg jeans. Deck pulled up a chair, turned it around, and sat so that his legs straddled it on either side and he could rest his chin on top of it.

Div leaned against the shelf, running a fingernail over the new CDs. "We heard you play Johnny's song again." She looked over at Taj. "You okay?"

Taj nodded. Her friends knew she was taking Johnny's disappearance pretty hard. The four of them had been a tight unit for a while. Before Johnny had become too famous, they had DJed parties together, calling themselves the MiSTakes as a joke on their TAP page, but the name stuck. The four of them were a team. Double-dating at Mel's Diner. Practicing tricks on the library steps, Johnny doing a perfect ollie on a twelve-step that got the other skaters clapping hands. Executing midnight missions where they pulled out all the skate-stoppers that party-pooper cops put up over all the best concrete ramps in the city.

"Check out what we got the other day," Div said, holding up a new Palm Treo, the latest version. "Neat, huh?"

"And look," Deck said, pointing at his shoes. "Nike SBs!"

"No way!" Taj said. She grabbed one of his ankles to take a closer look. SBs were the line's skateboard shoes, and Deck had them in hemp canvas. Taj knew the company had only made 420 pairs, and the entire inventory had sold out in half an hour. The shoes were an instant collectible—Japanese bidders paid thousands of dollars on eBay to acquire them. Taj had lusted after those shoes for ages. It hurt to see them on Deck's Bigfoot-size feet.

"TAP?" Taj asked.

"Where else?" Div grinned. "Not bad, eh?"

This was the deal. When you joined TAP, one of the privileges of membership was that you could put up a wish list—from Amazon, eBay, wherever. You could wish for almost everything online now, from cashmere sweaters to cars. Stuff you wanted to buy but couldn't afford. Stuff you wanted. Everyone did it.

The more friends you accumulated on TAP, the more stuff you got from your wish list. You didn't have to participate in the wish-list program, but once you did, you had to abide by its rules. Johnny had decided to sign up when he'd joined, but Taj hadn't. He'd told her about all the free stuff he'd received, but she didn't believe it until he showed her the custom-made thousand-dollar synthesizer someone had sent him. Johnny didn't have the money for anything like that. When Johnny's TAP friends reached epic proportions, stuff started arriving by the truckload.

And all you had to do was buy someone else

something from their wish list: a book, a CD, whatever. The site would send you their name, address, and a reminder, but here was the genius of it—you only had to get stuff for the people who'd joined TAP before you did. Everyone on TAP was assigned a number, from one to seven million (or however many members there were now); the smaller your number, the higher you were in the gifting hierarchy. The higher up you were, the more expensive an object you could expect to get. The lower you were, the more expensive a gift you had to buy in order to move up in rank. You didn't have to buy stuff for anyone who joined *after* you.

Taj still thought it was a little creepy getting stuff from people you didn't even know. But Div and Deck relished it. They kept putting up more and more expensive stuff—a fifteen-hundred-dollar digital camera for Deck, a Jimmy Choo bucket bag for Div— just to see how far they could push it. So far they'd received everything they'd asked for. Div said it didn't seem quite fair, having to buy some kid a CD and getting a two-hundred-dollar spa certificate in return, but then that was just the other kids' fault for not knowing how to "use the system."

Joining TAP was like having Christmas every day. And all you had to do was get more and more friends to join, and get them approved by two other people above you, which was easy enough, since Deck and Div were social-minded creatures who didn't mind accumulating e-mail addresses and asking total strangers to join TAP. And everyone usually got in. Usually. Although there had been a few blackballs lately, and rumor had it that membership would be restricted soon. TAP was quickly becoming an elite club.

"So, TAP party tonight, yo," Deck said. "We going?"

"We've never missed one yet," Div pointed out.

"I don't know . . . you guys sure you want to go?" Taj asked.

"What else is there to do?" Deck said in a reasonable tone. He was right. Even though the city was full of nightclubs and bars and all sorts of amusements, TAP parties provided something extra. It was all kids their age, for one. She and Div didn't have to worry about having gross older guys make passes at them, or hoping that their fake IDs would get them into the Dime this time, or having to pay a thirty-dollar cover at the door of Mood and then fifteen bucks for a watery drink.

TAP parties only cost twenty a head, and that came with all the TAP you could drink, and they usually had pretty good music or a band. Plus, there was the ritual. No one ever talked about it outside of TAP, but that was the big draw of the parties.

Taj put on the last song. The song she'd played as a sign-off ever since she'd taken over the show. Pink Floyd's "Wish You Were Here." Maybe if Johnny was out there, he was listening, and he would come home.

Taj's cell phone rang. "Sutton," she mouthed to let Div and Deck know who was calling. "Hey, guy."

"TajMahal," he greeted her. "My favorite MiSTake. You coming to my party tonight?"

"Wouldn't miss it for the world."

"Good."

"Did you see? Johnny hit number one in the UK, Germany, and the Netherlands. You know there's a role-playing game based on him in Brazil?"

"Are you serious?"

"Aren't I always?"

"Wow."

"Wow is right."

"Too bad he's not here to enjoy it," Taj said bitterly. She fought off the now nagging suspicion that Sutton had had something to do with Johnny's disappearance. Why would Sutton do that to his star? It was paranoia on her part.

"How do you know he's not enjoying it, wherever he is?" Sutton asked in a reasonable tone.

Melissa de la Cruz

"Whatever."

"So swing by about one a.m.; that's when it really gets going. It's 3500 Benedict Canyon. You'll be on the list plus two; I assume Tweedledee and Tweedledum are coming with."

"Fuck you, Sutton."

"Anytime, Taj. Anytime."

welcome to TAP.COM

| :OM | BROWSE | :EARCH | :NVITE | :ILM | :AI | :LO |
| FAVORITES | :ORUM | :ROUP | :VENTS | :IDE: | :US: | CLASSIFIEDS |

TAPPED IN....

Your news.
Your space.
Your funeral.
Put up
your stuff,
your videos,
your pics,
your photos,
your music.
Whateva
you gots for
us, we're
into it.

MEMBERSHIP IS FREE.
RESPECT IS NOT.

You are logged in as:
NickH3112.
If you are not
NickH3112, **click here.**

View my pics/videos:

TAP REQUESTS:
Mrniceguy8311, Sherman Oaks
[Approve] [Disapprove]

JuliaD1394, Venice Beach
[Approve] [Disapprove]

TAPPED IN . . . The latest news from your world

Member Login:

SCREEN NAME☆

PASSWORD☆

★
search TAP

COMMENTS

CRASHMCK542: HAVE A DAMME FINE DAY!! **[Click to link]**

MaxitotheMax13: hi sweetie! see you at the house,
don't be late!

HenryW8776: yo check out the disco-dancing Asian dude
in the speedo. LOL. **[Click to link]**

Shrminator4876: DUH . . . DEERRRRR . . . wazza???

Jennycake10485: sweet nicky . . . this cake is
moist!!!

[Add Comment] [Delete Comment]

★ [Click to Search for Friends] [Hot New People] [TAPPED IN Archives] ★

NICK CHUCKLED AS READ THE USUAL ONLINE
detritus. He took another slurp from the Red Bull can.
His third of the evening and already his heart was
beating too fast, and he was starting to get an awful
headache—kind of like the one he got when he tried
Viagra with Maxine that one time and his head
throbbed for hours. But in perverse fashion he relished the pain. Part of him felt like he deserved it.

There wasn't as much activity on TAP as he would
have liked, since it was a Saturday and most of his
real friends were actually out doing things rather than
typing in front of their computers—Nick still thought
of people whose names and phone numbers were
listed in his Motorola SLVR as "real" and those who
only existed online as not quite worthy of the title.

Nick listened to the DJ filling in for Johnny Silver—TAP said it was his girlfriend—on the radio for a while, liking the sound of her voice, letting the music she'd picked out for the evening lull him into something approaching sleep, when the back door suddenly opened.

"Hooo-rah!"

Nick shook his head. "I knew I should never have given you our security code."

Eric gave Nick one of his trademark manic-guy grins. "But I'm part of the family!" he protested, jumping up on the counter and slapping his palms together.

"Heard about you and Maxi. Sorry, bud," Eric said, attempting to look sympathetic, even though he'd told Nick on many an occasion to "dump the fucking bitch."

"Yeah, you and the rest of L.A.," Nick said, indicating the computer screen.

"Good news travels fast," Eric noted.

"Where've you been all night?" Nick asked, getting up and throwing Eric a can of Red Bull.

Eric popped the top and guzzled. "Vodka?"

"In the freezer."

While Nick watched Eric mix the toxic concoction, Eric told him about his evening. "Had dinner with the 'rents at Chow's, then went up to Malibu with a bunch of girls from Marymount—some friend having a beach party—but it was lame, so I got out of there, bummed around a bit looking for some party up in Temescal—couldn't find it. so then decided to look you up, since I heard Maxi dumped your ass—thought you might need cheering up. Stopped by my man first," he noted, holding up a baggie of pot, "and here I am."

"You were in Malibu *and* the Palisades?"

Like most Angelenos, Eric had essentially spent the evening in his car.

Eric shrugged. "No traffic. Got here in half an hour."

"The way you drive," Nick said, shaking his head.

Eric leaned over and checked out Nick's computer screen. "Ooh, can I check my page? Got a hottie from Ventura who said she'd send pics in a thong. Sick."

"Go ahead."

Eric called up his page; jumbled graffiti scrawl in the background made it hard to read, but it was easy to make out the premiere picture of Eric flying through the air on his snowboard, right before he broke his knee last year. "No new comments. Oh well." He got up from the computer and started walking around the kitchen in circles, attempting a succession of hip-hop dance moves.

"So, whatcha gonna do, just hang here all night?" Eric finally demanded, having exhausted his repertoire of pop and locks.

"Pretty much."

Eric made a face. "No way. Saturday night, kid. We need to bust outta here. Cruise Sunset. Pick up some shorties. Know what I'm sayin'?" Like many of the kids at school, Eric spoke in a semi-ironic but at the same time completely earnest affectation of hip-hop patois.

The tirade continued. "What you gonna do, watch *SNL*? Surf TAP? Give me a break. C'mon, let's go."

Eric took the wheel on his dad's vintage Bugatti, Nick riding shotgun, and they zoomed down the hill toward the Strip.

Sunset Boulevard stretched from the crowded Santa Monica beaches all the way to the East L.A. barrios. Not that Nick had ever even set foot in East L.A. To be honest, he wasn't even sure exactly where it was. Somewhere past downtown?

They looped around for the third time down the half-mile stretch of Sunset between Fairfax and La Cienega, Nick chuckling as Eric flashed a finger at the NO CRUISING signs that were posted every block. Traffic was a crawl, drivers leaning on their horns, checking one another out behind the wheel—open-top convertibles the only way to roll, as white-shirted valets wielding glow sticks directed motorists to their parking lots, the prices escalating as they neared the hotels, nightclubs, and restaurants that made Sunset such a popular destination.

Eric drove one-handed, his left arm gesturing toward the teeming crowds of people standing in line outside the velvet ropes in front of Chateau Marmont, Sky Bar, and the Standard. He was talking a mile a minute about the advantages and disadvantages of each nightclub. "We could hit Marmont before it gets crowded, or do Key—I heard the Arcade Fire is playing a secret set at about one a.m. The Standard's pretty over; they let everyone in."

Nick grunted, not particularly interested in any of it. It was always the same—the same people at the parties, the same people at the clubs; he'd even found himself having the same conversation with the same person the other weekend. Comparing workouts. Snore. There just had to be more to life than scoring a cabana at the Roosevelt and watching underage actresses push one another into the pool. Right?

He fiddled with the side mirror, taking note of the girls walking the sliver of sidewalk from club to club. They were uniformly tan, thin, and pretty with generic all-American actress/model features, dressed in skimpy, barely-there tops and even smaller skirts, and they teetered on strip club–worthy stilettos. It was true what they said about L.A.: There were so many pretty people, even pulchritude became boring. His thoughts wandered back to the girl he'd seen at Johnny's concert. The one with the ebony-black hair and the weird-ass getup. Now, there was a girl who didn't look like anybody else.

His head swam from the bright neon lights, the large Absolut billboard bearing down on him oppressively. The energy he'd felt back at the house was starting to ebb, and he suddenly wished he'd just stayed home. The fight with Maxine had drained him of any enthusiasm. *How could she?* he thought, not for the first time. He could live with a bruised ego, but public humiliation was another thing entirely. She'd made him look like a cuckold, a chicken; it was all over TAP. Everyone would know. Correction: Everyone knew. He didn't want that to bother him, but it did.

"Hey, man, do you think we could just . . . ," Nick said, knowing it was already too late.

"Here we be," Eric said as he pulled into the Mondrian's driveway, through the oversize walnut doors. Eric tossed the keys to the valet, and Nick reluctantly followed him into a blindingly all-white lobby that was reminiscent of the last scene in *2001: A Space Odyssey*—a surreal, clinical space full of white leather and glass. Eric sauntered—swaggered—up to the velvet rope that separated the public areas from the private.

A tall, bald man—one of the most famous door-men in Hollywood, who went by the one-word moniker Disco—waved them to the front of the line.

"Eric, my man," he said, grinning and pounding fists with Eric. "You guys need a table?"

"Please." Eric smiled, palming a hundred-dollar bill, which Disco pocketed smoothly.

Disco unhooked the rope and whispered to a pass-ing cocktail waitress to lead Eric and Nick to a choice table within the cordoned-off VIP section.

A few minutes later the two boys were lounging comfortably on a king-size mattress, sipping twelve-dollar cocktails and enjoying the panoramic view of the city that stretched from the ocean all the way to downtown. A fresh breeze blew the transparent linens on the cabana, and the air was sweetened with the scent of jasmine and hibiscus. Nick began to relax. Okay, so maybe he had been in a bad mood, but this wasn't so terrible, now, was it?

On a raised platform above the pool, the DJ spun

a sexy, lively mix of eighties dance music interspersed with twenty-first-century hip-hop, but almost no one was dancing. It was a strictly S&M crowd—stand and model—the pretty people posing as if ready for a Sante D'Orazio campaign.

Eric grinned hopefully at every pretty girl who walked by, to no avail, while Nick yawned into his shirtsleeve.

"She said to meet here, man, I swear. Ella—or was her name Ellen? I can't remember. Did she say Sky? Or was it Katana? Or Geisha House?" Eric began making a succession of phone calls to various friends to ascertain their location for the evening. The minute Eric arrived anywhere, he always felt like the action was somewhere else.

"Hey, guys," a voice cooed.

Salvation. A group of girls from school—all wearing midriff-baring tops, belly chains, and tight True Religion jeans—clustered around their table. Nick noticed that a couple of them had angel-wings tattoos somewhere on their bodies—Clarissa's was on the back of her neck, Allison's right above her bellybutton. The tattoos must be some kind of fad . . . something the cool kids adopted that spread to everyone else.

That was the way it had been, ever since junior high. For the girls, Tiffany bean necklaces, friendship string bracelets, Uggs, Crocs, those tiny tank tops with their names graffitied on the front. For the guys, Oakley rimless sunglasses, PlayStation Portables, old-school kicks. One day no one drank Red Bull; the next day everyone was mainlining it. What was in or out was adopted and discarded so quickly, it was hard to keep up. Nick always wondered who decided what was cool to wear, to drink, to buy. And why did everyone follow so slavishly?

"Omigod, aren't you so bored?" one of the girls— Ashley or Avery; Nick could never tell them apart— asked. "It's so lame tonight."

"Totally," Eric nodded.

"It's all, like, Valley trash. Disgusto." Another one nodded, flicking her hair over her tanned shoulders and turning up her nose at several revelers who were walking by the rope, sneaking a peek to see if there were any real celebrities in the VIP section (and looking disappointed when they didn't recognize anyone in Nick's party). "Go away!" she screeched to a hapless bystander. "Leave us alone!"

"Some people." Clarissa sniffed. "The absolute nerve."

"We're out. Going to this party up on Benedict— wanna come?" one of the girls asked.

"Amory's getting Tapped tonight."

"Shut up!" Clarissa frowned, punching her friend in the arm.

"Owee? What's the big deal? It's going to be hot."

The one named Amory, another lookalike blonde, looked from Nick to Eric and blushed, but said nothing.

"But isn't it at—?" One of the girls whispered to Eric, looking apprehensively at Nick.

Eric nodded soberly, but shrugged his shoulders— the international sign of *whatever*.

Nick barely paid attention to the conversation. As the group herded out to the valet stand, he was just glad to be in motion again.

Eric gripped him by the shoulder, trying to psych him up for the fun.

"C'mon bud, TAP party up in the hills. Remember what happened last time—whoa!" his friend cheered.

"No, what happened last time?" Nick asked, knitting his eyebrows together.

"Dude, I had such a great time, even I don't remember." Eric laughed.

Taj

THE FIRST TIME TAJ ATTENDED A TAP PARTY, SHE hadn't even known it was a TAP party. She and Johnny had received the invitation a little while after he'd posted a few of his songs online. They had gone out of boredom. *Why not?* he'd said one evening. *Let's go check it out.* It was a party up in Silver Lake, at a sprawling house that she recognized from half a dozen horror films.

They'd paid their twenty dollars and hung out. They only had kegs at the party back then; the promoters—whoever they were—hadn't introduced TAP the drink just yet.

It had sure looked just like any other party. Later she would remember the slight differences—the feeling of being watched, of being judged, the feeling that somewhere underneath the surface of the party a real event was going on, but that they were somehow missing out on it without quite knowing why.

She and Johnny had wandered through the house and found a door that looked like it would lead them outside, where they could at least sit by the pool. Taj opened it and was surprised to find a kid with a flashlight standing guard instead. "What's the word?" he asked.

From behind him Taj had seen a dark room filled with kids and heard the sounds of soft, intimate laughter and the thump of a dark, rich house-music beat, all bass line.

"Excuse me?" she'd asked.

"Sorry," he said. "Private party." He closed the door firmly in their faces.

Johnny and Taj looked at each other askance. When Johnny tried to open the door, it was locked. Huh. That was weird.

"Drug room?" Johnny asked, raising an eyebrow. Johnny had been practically straight edge back then. *Music is my life*, he'd said. *I don't need anything but my guitar to get high.*

"No, I didn't smell anything, did you?" she said. She hadn't glimpsed anyone surreptitiously angling a dollar bill up a nostril either. Besides, no one ever locked the drug room.

Just say no? Please. This was Los Angeles. Rehab was a mandatory pit stop between dropping out of high school and starring in a music video. Promises weren't a pledge to change; it was where you checked in after they kicked you out of Hazelden. Taj knew half a dozen kids who had burned out on dozens of illegal substances. She herself stayed out of the scene. Sure, she'd tried stuff—her motto was "Try everything once"—but Taj preferred clarity to oblivion. Like Johnny, she favored a natural high.

They'd left the party soon after, not quite being able to shake the feeling that they had been cheated of an experience.

The next week another invitation had arrived in their TAP in-boxes. At the bottom of the e-mail, a password had been supplied: Inferno. Maybe this meant they'd made the cut this time, Taj had thought.

Johnny had laughed it off, saying who did these people think they were, *the devillll*? Taj's curiosity was piqued against her better nature. She wanted to find out what it was all about.

Inferno had taken them inside the back room at a party up on Laurel Canyon. The room was pitch-black, and bodies were pressed tightly against one another in the dark.

"What's going on?" Taj whispered. "Is this all there is?"

A red light shone on one corner of the room, and a girl stood underneath it, holding what looked like a needle. The music started—the *bumf, bumf, bumf* of the techno beat—and the show began.

"Shhh," Johnny said, holding her hand tightly. "Let's wait and see."

They had done just that. Later, at the next party, they would even participate. Soon it got to be something that was simply part of their lives, part of the fabric of their existence. And just like the website, it was hard to stop once you'd started.

That evening as Deck drove them up through the curvy streets, Taj wondered if it was a good idea to stop by the back room this time. *Maybe tonight I won't,* she told herself. *Maybe tonight I won't do it.*

Benedict Canyon snaked up from Beverly Hills (where the street was simply called Cañon) all the way up to Bel-Air, where twenty- to thirty-thousand-square-foot villas—modern American palazzos—were the norm. It was a quiet, secluded, exclusive neighborhood; up here, Taj thought, even the air smelled fresher, as if even the ubiquitous Los Angeles smog wouldn't dare pollute the reaches of the lofty district.

Sutton's house was on a ridge high above the city. They drove up to a security gate, and Div quickly punched in the code. Hedges hid the house from the street, and as they drove up the winding private drive, it came into view: a large colonial mansion, intimidating in its size, with three-story marble columns, sparkling fountains, and lush landscaping. It looked like a resort or a hotel rather than a private residence.

They parked behind a long line of cars in the driveway, and walked inside to find the party in full swing. Groups of people were dancing wildly in the living room, the throbbing music piped through speakers that were invisibly installed in every corner of the house. There were kids everywhere—hanging off the balcony, assembled on the patio, smoking in the dining room, zoning out, and sitting down rolling cigarettes in the mazelike corridors that led to different wings of the house. Several tables by the side of the room were littered with open potato-chip and snack bags, half-empty handles of premium gin, vodka, rum, and whiskey, and plastic cups scattered every which way—dirty, clean, half-full, half-empty, full of cigarette butts.

Just your usual Bel-Air blowout. Nothing out of the ordinary here.

Taj surveyed the guests—she didn't see anyone she knew from school, but the slew of bodies parted as soon as the crowd noticed the three of them enter.

"That's Queen CoolGaze," someone whispered. A snarky website had given Taj that nickname after a photo of her and Johnny had run in the *Los Angeles Times* in an article about the burgeoning music revival. The hipster hottie who was reinventing rock and roll and his alterna-queen girlfriend.

Taj blushed. Those pictures were a joke. It was all fake. How could they not see it?

But even the high-maintenance high-school crowd had bought into it. The way they stepped back to let her pass was a sign of respect. She knew in an instant that these were private-school kids whose mommies and daddies toiled in the upper reaches of the entertainment industry and brought home money by the wheelbarrowful. The girls had hair the color of honey, smooth and buttery-perfect, golden caramel-delicious highlights painstakingly applied by a professional hand, and luminous skin that glowed from exotic spa treatments.

"We're going inferno," Deck said, thumbing toward the back of the house. Although the password changed every week, they always called it that after the first time.

"Already?" Taj asked.

"Yeah. I want to get my spirit on," Div said, her color high and her hands already shaking with excitement.

"Go ahead," Taj said. "I'll catch up later."

She wandered into the kitchen and picked up a beer from the Sub-Zero, forgoing the telltale red TAP punch that was available in a crystal bowl. She saw Sutton leaning by the counter; a tall, strikingly beautiful girl in a diaphanous silk dress, her shoulders tan and creamy, stood beside him. Taj remembered her from backstage at the Viper Room. He raised his glass and she walked over.

"Taj, do you know Maxine?"

"No," Taj said.

"Maxine, this is Taj. The one you've heard so much about. Johnny Silver's muse."

"I heard you're the one responsible for all of his songs," Maxine said.

Taj raised her eyebrow and looked at Sutton. What had Sutton told her? But Sutton looked blank.

"Thanks," Taj said icily, living up to her nickname. "Sutton, you haven't heard from him?"

"I told you, Taj, the minute I do, I'll let you know. I'm sure our Johnny's just, you know, hanging out somewhere."

For some reason this caused Sutton's date to giggle uncontrollably.

"Great party," Taj said, for conversation's sake.

"You going in?" he asked, nodding his head toward the back room.

"Later," she said.

"That's my girl." Sutton smiled.

"A lot of new people here," Taj said, surveying the crowd. God, and some of those kids looked really young—fourteen, thirteen, even.

Sutton nodded. "Word's spreading. That's the way we like it."

Taj took her leave and walked around the party. *I won't do it tonight. I won't. I won't.* But she found herself in front of the door anyway. And when the kid with the flashlight asked for the password, she gave it up willingly.

She walked inside the dark room, smelled the pheromones from the people around her, the woody, cloying smell of incense. She unzipped her jacket and stripped down to a thin black tank top. They were playing a track from Johnny's album. Someone handed her a plastic cup. Oh, well. What could it hurt. It was all-natural. Organic. It was good for you. It made you feel good. She drank it, savoring the familiar, sweet taste of TAP. No wonder Johnny had found it so alluring. This feeling of lightness, of joy, of ecstasy . . .

Johnny's voice was amplified on the speakers. It was almost as if he were there in the room with her.

She took off the tank top and stood there in her black lace bra. Then she unhooked the straps from behind and walked with her eyes closed into the crowd.

It was time for the ritual.

Nick

"I TOLD YOU, I'M LEAVING."

"Aw, c'mon."

"No."

"Don't be a wuss."

"Dude, just shut up."

"You shut up."

Nick shook his head. He should have known. The minute they drove up Benedict and pulled into the driveway, he realized how incredibly stupid he had been. *Some TAP party in Benedict Canyon.* Yeah, right. How could he have forgotten? Maxine had been talking about it all week.

Eric, that traitor, had taken him to one of Sutton's parties.

Sutton Werner was famous for his TAP events.

They were at different locations every time—once on his father's yacht in Marina del Rey, another time in an abandoned castle high up in the Silver Lake Hills. Every other Friday of the month, just like clockwork.

No one knew much about him; even though he was a perennial boldfacer in the "Tapped In" column, his personal TAP page contained the bare minimum of information, and he hardly ever updated the contents, nor did he allow friends to leave comments. It was like he'd come out of nowhere but was everywhere, so suddenly you couldn't escape him.

Nick remembered him vaguely from sixth grade. A wimpy little guy who wore glasses and carried an inhaler. Sutton's family had moved back east, but now they were back, and the asthmatic nerd had transformed himself into a popular partymonger. Sutton was a strange character—he wore ascots underneath his polo shirts, carried a silk handkerchief in his pocket, and had adopted the habit of looking as if he were peering at the world with the help of a monocle.

In any other school, in any other city, he would have been laughed at, mocked, shoved against the lockers, beaten within an inch of his life.

But in Los Angeles? At Bennet Prep? He was a

beloved character. A worshiped oddball. The secret to his popularity? An empty house, perennially absent parents, and keys to the most well-stocked liquor cabinet in the 90210 zip code. And the fact that his father helmed the biggest music label in the industry.

Nick had been to several of Sutton's parties, which were heavily promoted on TAP and linked to the site in some way—dozens and dozens of party pictures were posted on the site after each event. Photos of good-looking kids in various states of undress, but never so obscene as to be actually raunchy; Paris Hilton stepping out of a Ferrari in a miniskirt was more pornographic than anything TAP published. The appeal lay in the cooler-than-thou attitudes presented, the bizarre hairstyles, the outrageous fashion and the secretive air. Johnny Silver, with his thick white bangs that covered half his face, and his hyper-skinny frame in those tight black T-shirts and peg-leg jeans. The girls with their pin-curled hair and candy-red lips wearing fingerless gloves and peekaboo shirts. Even the fashion magazines had become hip to the phenomenon, and reported that TAP looks were being copied from Tokyo to Reykjavík. Johnny Silver and Queen CoolGaze clones multiplying across continents.

Melissa de la Cruz

Nick didn't have anything against Sutton, except for the fact that the guy had somehow misplaced his hands down Nick's girlfriend's shirt the other week. Nothing personal.

He had to get out of there. He was sure Maxine was somewhere on the premises, and he had to leave before he saw her.

"Later," he said, slapping Eric on the back.

"Dude, man, don't be like that," Eric pleaded. "Chill out—the guy may be a pretentious jackass, but the jackass's bar is stocked with 141 proof."

Nick just shook his head. "See ya."

"How are you getting home?" Eric yelled. "You don't have a car!"

Nick was making his way through the crowd, trying to get to the front door, when he noticed someone familiar. The curly blond hair, the jean jacket, the multitude of rubber bands on her wrist. Did Sutton know eighth graders were crashing his events?

"Hey, Fish!" he called. But the music was so loud she didn't answer, didn't even hear him.

He fought his way through. Her bright curly head was walking farther and farther into the party, and he followed her. This was no place for a kid. And even though Fish was precocious, she was still his baby stepsister. How did she even find out about this?

Fish was with those new friends of hers, and the group made its way to a back door. The door was opened a crack, and then he saw his sister and her friends walk inside.

He walked up just as the guy was closing the door.

"What's the word?" the kid with the flashlight asked, shining the beam right into Nick's face and making Nick blink in annoyance.

"Huh?"

"Sorry. Private party." The kid started pulling the door shut. Nick put a hand on the door.

"C'mon, my kid sister's in there."

"Sorry, brah. Boss man says no word, no entry."

A slip of a girl passed through from the other side. "Thanks, Charlie." She glanced at Nick, who was smiling in an amused fashion. It was the same girl from backstage at Johnny's concert. The one with the shiny black hair and the shy smile. The one whose face he couldn't stop thinking about, even as he'd been arguing with Maxine earlier that evening.

"We have to stop meeting this way," Nick said.

She looked up. "Do I know you?"

"No," he said. "We almost met—the night of

Johnny's concert? Me, the one without a backstage pass? Toe crusher?"

The girl's eyes cleared. She was drenched in sweat, her tank top plastered to her small frame. She was holding her leather jacket in her arms and she looked nervous.

"Oh, yeah." She smiled.

"Taj, do you mind?" the kid on guard said, as he closed the door firmly behind him.

"What's going on in there?" Nick asked.

"Oh, you don't want to know," she said, pursing her lips. "You're not missing out on anything, believe me."

Nick nodded. It was always some stupid thing. Like in sixth grade when people started being secretive about what went on behind closed closet doors; he finally found out it was just about kissing a girl, and he'd already done that. He'd been worried at first, but he relaxed. It was probably just some extreme version of a VIP room, and he'd been inside many VIP rooms. Nothing special ever went on in there. He relaxed.

He looked at her. She was really pretty. She wasn't wearing the glasses this time, and her skin looked translucent. What they called a regulation hottie, except there was nothing standard about her.

"You're Johnny Silver's girlfriend," he said suddenly. So that's why she looked so familiar. "The one with all those pictures on TAP. You're in the MiSTakes. You guys DJed at one of my friends' parties once."

"I have a name," she said coyly. "I'm Taj. Well, Tatiana, really. But no one calls me that."

"Taj . . . you do the show, right? On the college station?" Nick said, walking in step with her as they made their way through the crowded party.

"Yeah."

"I'm Nick. Nick Huntington."

Taj grinned. "Hey, you were the guy who called tonight. Is your name really Nick Nick?" she teased.

He blushed, jammed his fists into his trouser pockets. God, he could be such a nerd sometimes.

"I'm just teasing," she said slyly. "Walk me out?"

"Sure."

THE BOY SEEMED NICE ENOUGH. THE PREPPIE. ONE OF
Sutton's friends, most likely. She would let him walk
her out, and then she would disappear. The ritual was
a joke. She shouldn't have joined in; she knew that
now. It was too weird with Johnny gone, without him
looking out for her. It was scary—she didn't know
how Div and Deck could do that. It was all in good fun
at first, but now it was getting way too serious. It
wasn't what it was supposed to be anymore. There
were too many kids in there who just watched and
didn't participate. Too many boys who were there for
the wrong reasons. It wasn't about that, she'd wanted
to scream.

And the girl who'd gotten Tapped that night. She
looked like she was about to faint when she saw the

needle. The fear in her eyes! That had been painful to watch. And it wasn't supposed to be painful . . . it was supposed to be holy. A divine experience, shared with those who felt the same as you.

She'd only stayed for a few minutes, and then she'd had to bail. She didn't want to bump into Sutton again. He'd only convince her to stay. *Give it another chance. Let the Spirit move you.*

Just keep talking to the cute boy, she told herself. He wasn't one of the chosen. He didn't have the password. He didn't make the cut. She wondered why—he was handsome enough, surely. But those were the unwritten rules of TAP. Some people got in; some people didn't. She guessed he was one of those kids who just didn't get it. He was nice enough to offer her a ride home, but she told him all she needed was a ride down to Sunset.

"Oh man," the boy—Nick (he had a name)—was saying. "I totally forgot. I didn't drive."

"That's all right," Taj said. A Bel-Air preppie with no wheels? "You know how to ride one of these?" she asked, finding her board against the wall in the entrance hall. She handed him Deck's Osiris.

"A little. When I was a kid."

"I'll loan it to you. My friend won't mind. We could skate down the hill, then I could catch the bus home."

"The bus?" Nick smiled. It occurred to Taj that

he'd probably never heard of anyone actually taking the bus, let alone admitting it. *Well, welcome to my life,* she thought.

"Yeah."

"I think we can do better than that," Nick said.

"What are you thinking?" she asked. They walked companionably to the front gate, each of them holding a skateboard.

"Dude, not like that," Taj said. "You can't hold it like a briefcase."

"What?" Nick asked.

"Hold it here, by the lip, see? The top of the board?" Taj said, showing him. "Only amateurs hold it to the side, like you're doing. Dead giveaway. I can't be seen with anyone like that."

"Oh, no?"

"Nope. And don't hold it by the truck either," Taj said, pointing to the wheelbase. "Only gutter punks do that. It's a board, not a weapon. When you hold it by the truck it looks like you're planning to pound someone with it."

"Maybe I am." Nick smiled. *He is really hot,* Taj thought.

"Okay, whatever you say," he said.

They'd made it out to the gravel path when they were stopped at the exit by the same girl who'd been hanging on Sutton's arm earlier that evening. Maxine something. The one who'd made that comment about Taj being responsible for Johnny's songs. But the girl wasn't paying any attention to her. She was looking only at Nick.

"Sweetie."

Taj noticed Nick flinch.

"Maxine."

"Can we talk?"

Taj held up her hands. *Go ahead. Don't worry about me,* her shoulders communicated. She was cool, although she felt an instant flash of jealousy when she picked up on the tension between her new friend and Sutton's girl. But really, what was it to her? He was just a boy she'd met that night. Not even her type. Too clean-cut. Too rich. Yes, you could be too rich, in Taj's book. Look at what all that money did to Johnny. None of it good.

"Taj, hold on. Will you wait?" Nick asked, giving her back the board.

Taj gave Maxine a cool up-and-down. Queen CoolGaze indeed. "Only for a minute."

Nick

MAXINE LED HIM TO A QUIET CORNER ON A STONE bench behind the hedges at the side of the house. "What's the deal with you and Lady ColdFish?" she asked.

"Nothing. I just met her tonight," he said. "Why do you care?"

"Believe me, I don't," Maxine retorted.

Nick looked up to see the face he had so recently adored—those almond-shaped eyes, those full, rosebud lips, that upturned nose, that mole by the side of her left cheek; he d loved that mole most of all—and he felt . . . confused. Numb.

"Nicky," Maxine sighed. "Can we talk?"

She traced her fingers on his arm, her touch making his stomach leap in a thousand different directions.

He refused to look at her, but he didn't get up off the bench, either.

"It's all a mistake . . . there's nothing between us. Sutton . . . I think he was drunk—he, like, came on to me backstage. It was a mistake. I didn't know what he was doing. You know I'd never do anything like that. . . . Don't listen to any of the garbage on the Web, baby—I love you . . ."

Nick shook his head. If she wasn't with Sutton, why was she at the party? What did she want from him?

Maxine placed her hands on each side of his face, "Look at me."

He did and sighed.

"Don't do this to us."

For a year now they had been an "us." He still remembered how it started—they'd just hung out in a group, the guys from the soccer team and the Beverly Hills girls, and Maxine had just been one of them. She was the new girl; she'd only transferred to Bennet Prep earlier that year. Rumor had it she'd grown up in Riverside of all places, and that her mother had remarried very, very, very well.

"Look, I gotta go," he said, gently taking her hands away. "Maxine, like I told you this evening, we're over."

"No one dumps me," Maxine said, gritting her teeth, her eyes narrowing. "No one leaves me, ever. Got it?"

"Well, there's always a first time," Nick pointed out.

"You'll regret this," she warned.

Nick shrugged his shoulders. "What's your problem?"

"You know," Maxine said, her exquisite face twisted in a cauldron of hatred, "Sutton was right about you. You're nobody. You don't even know half of what's going on all around you. I don't even know why I wasted my time."

"Good-bye, Maxi," Nick said. "I'll see you at school."

"I'll see you in hell."

Nick shook his head. He'd had his share of bitter breakups, but Maxine was by far the most psycho. Why did she even care? It wasn't like she was so into him, after all; she was the one who was cheating. But there were girls like Maxine who could never take rejection. Not even when they had caused it. They believed they deserved to be loved, to have everything in spite of their actions. Or that their actions had no consequences.

He was sick of it. He was tired of being a chump.

The good guy. The one who turned a blind eye to her indiscretions. This time she had gone too far. There was a picture on the Web for everyone to see. His pride had been hurt. And maybe his heart, as well. He wasn't sure. Was it even possible to fall in love at seventeen? He wasn't a cynical guy, but he was pretty sure what he and Maxine had had wasn't love.

He walked over to where Taj was waiting patiently. "Everything all right?" she asked, noticing the dark flush on his cheeks.

"Everything's perfect," he said. "Now, I'm a bit rusty, but you wanna skate down the hill and I'll call you a cab? It's on me. Don't worry about it. Can't have pretty girls like you walking around town at three a.m. by themselves. It's not safe."

"Pretty girls?" Taj smiled.

"Very," Nick said, smiling back. Somehow, seeing Taj had taken the sting out of the conversation with Maxine.

She taught him how to balance on the board, and together they coasted down the hill, all the way back to Sunset, where Nick, as promised, called her a cab and gave the driver a twenty to take her home.

"What are you doing next week?" Taj called from the backseat, while Nick stood on the curb.

"I don't know. You tell me."

"Well, maybe you're having dinner at my house on Friday night. I make a mean *kapusta*. And if you don't know what that is, you'll have the privilege of finding out."

"Okay, then," Nick agreed. "I'll call you, at the station."

"Do that."

The cab drove off, and Nick stood on the sidewalk, watching until it disappeared over the hill. He felt lighter and more energetic than he had in a long time. He also noticed that his headache was gone. Dinner at her house. Who ever invited anyone to dinner anymore? He couldn't remember the last time a girl had cooked for him. Maxine ate exclusively at restaurants where celebrity presence was guaranteed. If there were no paparazzi idling on the sidewalk, she wasn't interested. Maxine . . . Nick shook his head. Already it felt as if they had broken up last year instead of just several hours ago.

welcome to
TAP.COM

HOME   BROWSE   SEARCH   INVITE   FILM   MAIL   BLOG
FAVORITES   FORUM   GROUPS   EVENTS   VIDEO   MUSIC   CLASSIFIEDS

TAPPED IN....

Your news.
Your space.
Your funeral.
Put up
your stuff,
your videos,
your pics,
your photos,
your music.
Whateva
you gots for
us, we're
into it.

MEMBERSHIP IS FREE.
RESPECT IS NOT.

Member Login:

SCREEN NAME☆

PASSWORD☆

search TAP

You are logged in.
TAP.COM

DV844Wish List
☑ Palm Treo
☑ Jimmy Choo bucket
  bag
☑ MAC makeup Kit
☑ Marc Jacobs quilted
  handbag
☑ Tsubi jeans
☑ Skateboard
☑ Snowboard
☑ $100 deposit to
  PayPal account

RickDeckard45
Wish List

☑ Nike SBS 420 (Hemp)
☑ Skateboard
☑ Backpack
☑ Nikon camera
☑ Snowboard
☑ Patek Philippe watch
☐ Sony PSP
☐ $100 deposit to PayPal
  account

View more wish lists?
[Search]

COMMENTS

[Click to Search for Friends] [Hot New People] [TAPPED IN Archives]

Nick

THE PHONE WOKE NICK WITH A START THE NEXT
morning, bright and early at eight o'clock. It was a
shrill, electronic ring which echoed throughout the
ten-thousand-square-foot house and bounced off the
marble floors.

"Helllo?" Nick grumbled, still underneath his pillow.

"May I speak to Miss Langley?" a crisp voice
asked.

"You mean Mrs. Huntington," Nick corrected. He
turned and buried himself under the comforter. He'd
forgotten to draw the curtains the night before, and
the sun was streaming into his bedroom.

"No, a Miss Langley. A Miss . . . er . . . Fish
Langley?"

"Fish? Who is calling please?" Nick asked sternly, tossing the pillow to the floor and sitting up finally. Might as well just get up; he'd never be able to get to sleep again, what with the light.

"This is Citibank. If you please, sir, we'd like to talk to her about her account," the caller said in slightly accented English. Nick pictured a hapless Indian clerk in Bombay reading from a script.

That was odd. They both had debit privileges on their parents' Citibank checking accounts, but if the bank wanted to talk to an account holder, why would they want to talk to Fish?

"Hold on," Nick said. He pressed the intercom. "FISH! PHONE FOR YOU!"

There was no answer from Fish's room. She was probably ignoring him. It really was too early to deal with anything like this.

"I'm sorry, she's not here right now," Nick said.

"Thank you very much, sir. We will try again later."

Nick put the phone back on its base. Maybe the bank was trying to sell something—they always were.

He yawned and decided to take a morning run.

When he returned from a slog up and down the canyon, sweaty and refreshed, he noticed that Rosa, their housekeeper, had already set up a breakfast buffet in the kitchen. He picked a croissant from the tray and tore it in half, stuffing it into his mouth.

"*Hola,*" he said. "Fish come down yet?"

"No, Mr. Nick. No Fish." Rosa shook her head.

Nick looked at the time. It was only ten o'clock. He'd give the kid till noon, then ask her if she knew anything about Citibank, and what she'd thought of the party the night before. She'd be thrilled to know he'd met Taj Holder—Fish had Web shots of Taj in a series of outfits taped to her wall. Fish was a big MiSTakes fan, and she played Johnny Silver's record around the clock.

Saturday at the Huntington household was usually quiet. If Dad and Evelyn were home, which they weren't, they would be out at the country club by now for a tennis tournament. Nick checked the calendar by the phone. Dad was shooting in the Czech Republic. Evelyn was making a presentation in D.C. on global warming. Neither of them would be home for another week or two.

Thank God for Rosa. If it weren't for the housekeeper, who'd been nanny to both Nick and Fish, they would never have had a real home-cooked meal, let alone someone who remembered to sign them up for dental appointments and pick Fish up from acting class.

Nick made himself a plate of cold cuts and pastries, then took it up to his room.

A few hours later, Eric called to ask him if he wanted to drive up to Malibu for a party. "Man, what happened to you last night?"

"Nothing. I went home."

"Serious?"

"Yeah."

"Well, you missed out."

"Where were you?"

"You know there's this back room, right? At the party. Dude, I'm telling you, it's crazy in there. You've got to come with me next time."

"I tried. They wouldn't let me in. Said I needed a password."

"Oh. Right. Forgot about that. Didn't you get one in your in-box?"

"No."

"Oh."

There was an awkward silence.

"What goes on in there anyway?"

"Ah, it's nothing. Nothing to be worried about. I'm sure you'll get the password next time."

"Hey, did you see my sister in there, by the way?"

"Your sister—you mean Fish?"

"Yeah. I saw her go inside. They wouldn't let me follow her."

"I don't think I saw her," Eric said cagily. "It was really dark."

"Oh. Whatever."

"So you wanna go to the 'bu?"

"Sure."

When Nick left for the afternoon, Fish still hadn't emerged from her room. When he returned late that evening, the house was so quiet he decided she'd already gone to sleep. The next day was the same— Nick had to leave early for practice and didn't get home until late after hanging out with the team.

It wasn't until Monday night—three days later— when Fish didn't come home from school, that Nick finally realized something was wrong.

Fish had never come home on Friday night.

She was missing.

You are logged in as NickH3112. If you are not NickH3112 [click here](#):

NickH3112 has 148 TAP friends.

TajMahal22 has added you to her TAP Friends list.
Clarisssma, ashleyangel, hillaryious,
[click to see 8 more](#)
has deleted you from their friends list.

TAPPED IN . . . The latest news from your world

Saw **Maxine U.** and **Sutton W.** at the Neil Lane counter earlier. Heard she left with a nice pair of D-grade ICE. Nice.

[Four Comments] [Add a Comment]

bunnyficient215: aw, ain't young love sweet?

sailin'_away999: What up with her ex? Is he crying in his soccer cleats?

If_only_you_loved_me7588: I heard he's totally anti lately, as in anti-social. Haven't seen him ANYWHERE.

sucka_two107: too ashamed to show his face. Did you hear what he did at the party??? what a jerk!!! She's better off . . .

[Click to Search for Friends] [Hot New People] [TAPPED IN Archives]

TAPPED IN....

Your news.
Your space.
Your funeral.
Put up
your stuff,
your videos,
your pics,
your photos,
your music.
Whateva
you gots for
us, we're
into it.

**MEMBERSHIP IS FREE.
RESPECT IS NOT.**

Member Login:

SCREEN NAME☆

PASSWORD☆

search TAP

"IS THIS A NEW BOYFRIEND?" MAMA FAY ASKED,
pounding pieces of veal into paper-thin slices. The
force of her hammering shook the kitchen counter.

"No, Mama Fay, he's not my boyfriend," Taj said,
dipping the pounded veal into an eggy mixture and
then coating it in bread crumbs and flour. "We just
met last week. I told you, at a party in Bel-Air."

"Why not? He's not good enough for you, doll?"
Mama Fay fired up the stove and poured oil and butter
into a sizzling fry pan. When the oil began to bubble,
she picked up a cutting board full of onions and gently
eased them onto the surface.

The delicious smell of fried butter and onions per-
meated the air. "Hand me that cabbage for the
kapusta," Mama Fay ordered.

Taj made a face. "What if he doesn't like *kapusta*?" she asked, her nose wrinkling at the thought of eating the pungent cabbage and sauerkraut slaw. She'd only mentioned it to Nick as a joke.

"How can he not like *kapusta*?"

As a concession to Taj, Mama Fay was wearing what she called her Laura Bush outfit: a trim sweater set and a necklace of fake pearls. But that was as far as she would go—the pants were form-fitting and leopard-print. And Mama Fay had styled her hair into a towering beehive and had glued on her most abundant fake eyelashes, so that it looked like two spiders were attached to her eyes.

Taj set the rickety table in the alcove off the kitchen with three places. She didn't know why she had decided so impulsively to invite Nick over to dinner. Okay, so he'd paid her cab fare, but did she really owe him dinner? It had just come out of her mouth—wanna have dinner at my house?—before she could process what an invitation like that meant.

"What about the old boyfriend?" Mama Fay was asking. "The famous one. The one who went crazy and went to Africa."

"Who knows?" Taj shrugged. "I haven't heard from

him. Now they're saying he went to Tibet, to be with the monks."

"Monks? Why monks? My Lord, I can't see that boy with the monks."

Johnny had loved *kapusta*. He'd loved everything about Mama Fay, had even enjoyed hanging out at the cabaret. And Mama Fay and the drag queens had adored Johnny in return. So handsome! That hair— how can it be natural! Those eyes! They thought he was more beautiful than any boy they'd ever met.

Johnny had lapped up all the affection. He'd practically been part of the family. In fact, until all that stuff started happening with TAP, when he began getting big, and playing gigs, and then the record deal happened and he was so busy dealing with music execs he didn't have time to hang out—at least, that was his excuse; Taj knew that at that point there were other girls involved—until then, he was always hanging out at her house.

He didn't talk about his home life, but Taj figured there wasn't much to say. She'd seen the bruises on his arm from the beatings his stepfather administered, and as for his mom, according to Johnny she was so tired from working two jobs she never even noticed him.

Did they worry about him like she did? Were they proud of his album? Did they even care that he was missing? Had disappeared?

Taj went to the bathroom to check on her appearance. Nick was arriving soon. He'd sounded distracted when he called, but he'd promised he would be there tonight.

She was wearing a little plaid dress she'd hemmed to mini length, black stockings, and platform heels, and she had taken care to blow-dry her hair perfectly. *God, what do I care. He probably thinks I look really stupid.* But she applied a second coat of lip gloss anyway.

NICK PULLED UP TO THE ADDRESS TAJ HAD GIVEN him. It was in a desolate area of the Hollywood flats, next door to two empty lots. He noticed a couple of junkyard dogs sniffing around. His first thought was that the neighborhood was uglier and grittier than he had assumed, and the second was that he was a snob for thinking like that. He didn't like to think of himself as a snob.

The patch of garden in front of the house was full of weeds and rotting plastic furniture. Did Taj really live here?

He walked up to the door and rang the bell.

He heard some yelling from inside—"GET THE DOOR!" "GOT IT!" "JEEZ!"—and a few minutes later Taj was standing in the doorway.

She was wearing some kind of dress that skimmed her body and was cut short on the thigh. Nick thought she looked amazing, and he told her so.

"Yeah, I remember now—you're the one who thinks I'm pretty." Taj smiled. "Are those for me?"

"They're for your . . . uncle, actually," Nick said, handing over the vase of flowers he'd picked up from Eric Buterbaugh's Beverly Hills boutique earlier that afternoon.

"Aw, so sweet! Come on in," Taj said.

Nick ducked inside and was immediately struck by how cozy and delightful the bungalow looked with its comfortable couches and whitewashed floors. Not at all like it looked on the outside. Someone had picked out some nice things—the lamps were interesting and beautiful, and there were original prints framed all around.

A large woman (or a man dressed as a woman) walked out to the living room from the kitchen.

"You didn't tell me your friend was so handsome!" Taj's uncle beamed. "C'mon, give Mama a hug!"

Nick smiled nervously and allowed himself to be fawned over.

"Look," Taj said. "Flowers."

"Nice." Mama Fay nodded. "Thank you, my dear."

"C'mon," Taj said, pulling on Nick's arm. "Let me

give you the tour." Taj placed the flowers on a nearby side table.

"This is a cool house," Nick said, marveling at the family pictures and the wood-paneled den. He meant it too.

"It's so not. I bet our house could fit in one room of yours," Taj said, guessing correctly.

"Yeah, but it's a dollhouse. No one really lives there," Nick said, looking over all of Mama's old pictures from when she was a Marilyn Monroe impersonator, as well as all the tchotchkes in a glass case, souvenirs from when Mama Fay had traveled the world on her musical tours—miniature obelisks from Egypt, porcelain dolls from the Netherlands, painted fans from Japan.

"Are these your parents?" he asked, pointing to an old Polaroid of a young couple sitting on a bench, the Statue of Liberty in the background.

"Yeah, that's them. They're from New York. Their parents moved there from the Ukraine. They're both first-generation. They moved to L.A. before I was born."

"What happened to them?" They were a good-looking couple, Nick thought. He could see where Taj inherited her looks.

"They died in a car accident," Taj said. "It's kind of why I don't drive. I'm too scared."

Nick reached over and touched her hand. "I'm sorry."

"It was a long time ago. I don't even remember them. My first memory is of Mama Fay teaching me all the words to "I Will Survive." She raised me."

"Was he always like that?" he asked.

"You mean, in drag? Uh-huh. She was real pretty when she was younger." Taj picked up an old vinyl photo album from the bottom shelf and paged through it until she found what she was looking for. "Look. This is Mama Fay when she toured Asia." Mama Fay was dressed in a tight-fitting cheongsam and carrying a parasol.

"You know, in the eighties, when she went to Ukraine to visit her relatives, they asked her if she was an American celebrity. Mama Fay was going through her Cher phase."

"What did she say?"

"Yes, of course. Mama Fay's always been famous in her own head."

Nick could see that. There was a lot of love in the room. He thought back to the cold, empty house in Bel-Air. Where the only person who used the stove was the maid.

"I thought you were cooking."

"I helped—doesn't that count?" Taj grinned. She

Melissa de la Cruz

felt nervous and wasn't sure why. "Let's go out here."

Taj led him to the back door, to the patio where there was a tiny garden filled with bougainvillea and lavender jacaranda trees. The garden looked out at a view of the Capitol Records building. Hollywood Boulevard's bright lights beamed up to the sky.

"Isn't this such a great view? We moved here when I was eight. Before then we just lived out of hotel rooms, but Mama decided it wasn't good for me to be around all those nightclubs, and she decided to settle here, where my parents had lived."

She took a seat on the ancient swing and motioned for Nick to sit down next to her. He pushed off with his foot and rocked them back and forth. The night air buzzed with the sound of chirping crickets.

"It's so quiet."

"Yeah."

"You wouldn't think . . ."

"Wouldn't think what?" Taj asked, a little defensively.

"Nothing—it's just not how I expected it to be."

Taj relaxed.

"I'm sorry, I'm just a bit out of it . . . See, my sister's disappeared," Nick said. He'd been trying not to think about it for a few hours, but it was impossible. He was worried.

"What do you mean?" Taj asked, concerned.

"This is so jacked, but I didn't even notice until Monday. I mean, Fish keeps to her own schedule, and she goes in and out whenever she wants to. She's only thirteen, but . . ."

"Fish? You mean the kid who was in the paper today?" There had been another story, but this one was buried in the metro section. No longer headline news.

"Yeah."

"God, Nick, I'm so sorry. Don't you have to be at your house? If she calls?"

"My parents are there. I mean, my dad and my stepmom—Fish's mom. They were arguing about whether to report it, but I finally convinced them. They didn't see the need; I mean, she's done this before."

"Run away?"

"No. Just not tell us where she is. Last summer she went to visit her dad in New York without telling us, and we had no idea where she was for days. Evelyn just thinks she's at a sleepover or something. Although it's been a week, and we've asked all her friends and they all say the same thing."

"Which is?"

"The last time they saw her was at that party—

you know, the one up on Benedict Canyon. They all got separated when they went into that back room. And her friends said they don't know what happened; they think she took a cab by herself. She does that. I don't know what to think."

"Jesus."

"Taj, I have to ask you something."

"What?"

"What really goes on in that back room? I mean, do you think someone there could have hurt—"

"No!"

Nick watched as Taj bit her thumb.

"Look, I'm sorry, but I can't really say. But that's not the way it works," she said.

"What do you mean?"

She shrugged. "It's harmless. Nothing could have happened to her in there."

"I wish I could believe you."

"Nick . . ."

"What do you know about that guy who throws the parties?"

"Sutton? I don't know—he's just some rich kid, right? I thought he was a friend of yours." Taj shrugged.

"He's not. He goes to Bennet, but we're not friends."

"I don't know. I don't know much about him. Johnny—he was the one who dealt with Sutton, mostly." She pursed her lip and looked like she wanted to say more, but didn't.

Nick pressed his latest theory on her. "Don't you think it's a bit strange, Taj, how Johnny's disappeared? And now my sister? And what about all those kids in L.A. who are missing? Do you think TAP might have something to do with it?"

"The website?" Taj sounded incredulous. "You must be joking."

"I don't know. I'm just thinking aloud. I just find it odd that all these things have been happening. And I think it might all be linked to TAP."

"What makes you think so?"

"I don't know, I'm just guessing. Fish spent so much of her time online at that site, and then the parties are sponsored by them."

"The parties are totally separate," Taj said.

"Hey, why are you getting so defensive?" Nick asked, noticing how tense she suddenly looked.

"DINNER'S ON!" Mama Fay called from the kitchen.

"I'm not," Taj said, but it was obvious something was bothering her.

"You know, if you don't mind, I think I'll just go home. I'm really not that hungry."

She was hiding something from him, he could tell, and it made him angry. His sister was missing, after all. He needed all the help he could get.

Without another word, Nick stood up and left.

Taj

WHAT AN ASSHOLE, TAJ THOUGHT WHEN SHE HAD
to explain to Mama Fay that their guest had abruptly
departed for the evening, without sampling the
home-cooked dinner her uncle had prepared.

"I guess he doesn't like *kapusta*," Mama Fay joked.
She rubbed Taj's hair affectionately. "Don't sweat it,
pumpkin. Boys are sensitive creatures. What happened?"

She shook her head. "He's upset. His sister's
missing." She told Mama Fay what Nick had told her.

Mama Fay made a *tsk-tsk* sound. "So many kids
getting lost these days. A pity. You know, in my day
we'd all just run away to go to the East Village. That's
where we were. Your granny, she ran off to the Haight-
Ashbury. I'm sure that's all it is. They'll all come home

soon. You'll see. When they run out of spending money. But don't you go anywhere, doll."

They ate their dinner in silence.

Later that night, Taj dialed a familiar number.

"Speak."

"Hey, Div. Wanted to ask you a question."

"G'head."

"You know on Friday night?"

"Yeah."

"In the back room. Did anything . . . I don't know . . . did anything happen?"

Div hooted. "Lots of things happened. You know what it's like. By the way, why'd you bail so early?"

"Complicated."

"Anyway, why are you asking?"

"There were a bunch of young kids there—you know? Eighth graders?"

"Maybe. I didn't really notice."

"Anyway, one of them's missing. A friend of mine's sister."

"And this has to do with the back room why?"

"I know, I told him there was nothing there that would cause that . . . I mean, shit. You know? But I just thought . . . I don't know, if you'd seen anything weird."

"Everything's weird. That's the great thing about the ritual. You know that."

"Okay, then."

"Wanna know what we got this week?"

"What?"

"Plane tickets to San Francisco! Cool, huh? And Deck got this crazy expensive watch. Some kind of Swiss thing. Patek something. He saw it in some magazine and put it on his list."

"You guys are out of control."

Taj hung up the phone. She dialed another number.

"Hello, TajMahal," the voice drawled.

"Sutton. Wanted to ask you something."

"Sure, baby, anything for you. But in answer to your question, I have not heard from Johnny. I'm sorry. I think he's all right, though. I can feel it."

"It's not about Johnny."

"No?"

"What did you tell Maxine?"

"Maxine?"

"Yeah. About Johnny's songs."

"Nothing, baby. I just told her you inspired them. I mean, you did, didn't you?"

Taj exhaled. "You know, if it gets out, Sutton . . ."

"Trust me, baby, everything's cool. Trust Sutton. Johnny did. Aight?"

"There's some kid missing. Did you see the papers? It said she was last seen at your party, Sutton. At a TAP party. And all those other kids who've been reported lost were last seen at one of your events. What's the deal?"

"Saw it, sweetheart. Nothing to worry about. Lots of kids go to my parties."

"This one is different. It's a friend's sister."

"Who's the friend?"

"Nick Huntington."

Taj heard Sutton whistle between his teeth.

"Shut up, Sutton. Haven't you done enough to the guy?" Taj asked, meaning Maxine.

"Not nearly enough," Sutton grumbled. "Is that all?"

"No. I mean, yes. I mean . . . you will call me if you hear from Johnny, won't you?"

"Of course. Good-bye, Taj."

Click.

Nick

WHEN NICK ARRIVED HOME, HE IMMEDIATELY went to his room, turned on his computer, and logged into TAP. Something about what he'd said to Taj that night had bothered her. *What makes you think it's part of TAP?* There had to be something in that.

He studied the site intently and noticed something in the upper corner of his home page. A logo. Shaped like angel wings. He'd never noticed it before, but then he'd never really looked before. Like a lot of kids, he used TAP to get in touch with people, put up some fun stuff, but he never really thought twice about it.

TAP had always had a somewhat hokey feel—there were no ads on the front pages, and the whole site looked like something designed by your kid brother on Dreamweaver. It was part of its charm.

He clicked through the home pages of all his friends. Each one had the same angel wings in the upper left-hand corner. He checked blog pages, mail pages, video pages. There it was, over and over again. Right behind the "Welcome to TAP.com" box. Come to think of it, the logo looked a whole lot like the angel wings tattoos everyone was sporting. What gave?

Nick studied it thoughtfully. Then he sent an IM message to the one guy he was sure would know the symbol's provenance. Eric was always connected, he IMed from his cell.

Hunter1: Hey e, what up. Have you seen this before?

He cut and pasted the angel wing sign onto the screen.

crashnburn: looks like a logo

Hunter1: yeah I know it's a logo. see, it's in the upper left-hand corner of all TAP pages. Is it theirs?

crashnburn: dunno

Hunter1: doesn't YourPage own TAP?

crashnburn: Yar. but their logo is the little people all lined up.

Nick had seen that logo before—it was all over TAP as well. It looked like a bunch of restroom door icons lined up together. Seeing it always made him want to find a bathroom.

Hunter1: so what r u sayin

crashnburn: maybe someone else owns YourPage?

Hunter1: could u check it out?

crashnburn: Sure.

He waited a few minutes, clicked on a couple of music sites, read some gossip on TAP. Maxine was talking shit about him all over the Web. Ugh.

A few minutes later, there was a ping on his screen.

Instant Message from crashnburn: ACCEPT?

Nick clicked yes.

crashnburn: Found it.

crashnburn: YourPage is owned by Werner Records, the big music conglomerate.

Hunter1: You mean they bought out YourPage when it was getting big?

crashnburn: No. the opposite. They set up YourPage to put out TAP.

Hunter1: That's weird, isn't it? Didn't those two guys Jim Freestone and Mark Riley set up TAP at USC?

crashnburn: nope. looks like they were hired to start TAP. From the corporate docs I was able to hack.

Hunter1: Thanks 2. I owe you.

crashnburn: No worries. Hey, did you hear about the bear and the bunny shitting in the woods?

Hunter1: No. <groan>

crashnburn: mr. bear asks mr. bunny, mr. bunny do you find shit sticks to yr fur? mr. bunny says, why no, mr. bear. it doesn't.

Hunter1: uh-huh

crashnburn: so mr. bear picks up mr. bunny and wipes his ass.

Hunter1: classy, e. real classy.

crashnburn: i do my best. LOL. Hey, any word on your sister?

Hunter1: no. it sucks. rents think she's just pulling a 'fish.'

crashnburn: sorry bout that. sure she's fine.

Hunter1: hope so.

crashnburn: All right. Be strong. Later.

Hunter1: Bye.

Odd that one of the most popular websites online was actually created and owned by one of the biggest music conglomerates in the world. That certainly deviated from the standard Silicon Valley success story—two college kids set up a site and got all their friends to join, then their friends got all of their friends to join, and before you knew it, local newscasters were talking about how dangerous the site was, and there were hundreds of articles written about the safety of kids online, but by then the college kids had sold out and collected their millions.

Eric was telling him the complete opposite—that the company had hired two college kids to set up a site to front TAP.

But why?

welcome to TAP.COM

TAPPED IN....

Your news.
Your space.
Your funeral.
Put up
your stuff,
your videos,
your pics,
your photos,
your music.
Whateva
you gots for
us, we're
into it.

MEMBERSHIP IS FREE.
RESPECT IS NOT.

Member Login:

SCREEN NAME☆

PASSWORD☆

★
search TAP

You are logged in as
TajMahal22. If you are
not TajMahal22
click here:

TajMahal22 Top 5 Friends
"Jim" *JohnnyS11*
RickDeckard45 *DV844*

Move **NickH3112** to your Top 5 ?
[Approve] [Disapprove]

TAPPED IN . . . The latest news from your world

You searched for **"NickH3112"**
Displaying 1-5 of 3500 entries for **"NickH3112"**
Anon10: **Nick H** and **Maxi U**: hot new couple alert! Saw
them totally making out at the **[click to read more]**

Swede_swede39987: does anyone have any pics of
Nick H without his shirt? Can't find any and want to
[click to read more]

Disasterzone487: **Maxi U** is such a lucky gal. heard
Nick H planned the sweetest valetine's day for them at
[click to read more]

Breakdancefever321: spotted: **Nick H** with **Eric M** at the
Dime, at **Jessica S**'s table and **[click to read more]**

Miss_muffet765: who's coming to my party? EVERYONE.
Hello! **Nick H**, **Maxi U**, **Sutton W**, **Eric M**
[click to read more]

★ [Click to Search for Friends] [Hot New People] [TAPPED IN Archives] ★

Taj

GOD, THIS HOUSE WAS HUMONGOUS. IT WAS ALMOST
as big as Sutton's spread, if not bigger. How did people
even live in such vast palaces? Didn't it get lonely? Or
scary? She wondered what it would be like to wander
around those infinite rooms. She sat on the sidewalk
and waited for Nick to come home. She hadn't
thought of ringing the bell, being too shy to announce
herself. She was betting on catching him when he
came home from school.

Their conversation the other night was bothering
her, and she wanted to apologize, even if it was he
who had been rude. When Nick found her, she was
just sitting on the sidewalk, her board at her feet, like
a lost urchin.

"Taj?" he asked, rolling down the window to his

convertible. "What are you doing here?" He looked more than surprised. Maybe he'd thought after the stunt he'd pulled he would never see her again. But then, Taj wasn't like other girls.

"What does it look like? I'm having a chocolate chip cookie," she said cheerfully, holding aloft a damp bag of Mrs. Fields. When Nick still looked confused, she set him straight. "I've been waiting for you, what else? Took you long enough! Doesn't school let out at three?"

"I had practice. Why didn't you call me?"

"I would have, if I had your cell. And you guys aren't listed."

"Well, get in," Nick said, unlocking the door.

Taj jumped in. "Nice car." She whistled.

Nick drove them up the winding driveway.

Taj looked sideways at Nick, admiring his profile. If you'd told her a few weeks before that she would be hanging out with some Bel-Air preppie, she would have swatted you with her skateboard.

"Jesus. It looked huge from down the hill, but up close it's even more enormous."

"Yeah," Nick said, a little embarrassed. "It's been in my dad's family for years."

Taj shook her head. Nick parked the car in the garage and led Taj into the house through the kitchen.

Melissa de la Cruz

Nick excused himself to his room, citing a need to change out of his sweaty soccer uniform, while Taj looked around at the kitchen, admiring its immaculate emptiness, the appliances only peeking out from behind roll-down doors. The countertops, honed in onyx, didn't sparkle but glowed with a soft, calibrated light.

It was a beauty that she had only seen in the pages of glossy, oversized magazines. Flowers sat under focused spotlights, their petals and leaves stapled and arranged into elaborate shapes that contrasted the starkness of the modern kitchen.

She had been to her share of rich-kid parties, had seen these houses close-up—this was just as impressive as Sutton Werner's, if not more so. But she had never known anyone who actually lived in one of these houses; she had always thought of those people in the abstract. Sutton didn't count, somehow. He was just Sutton. But she was starting to think of Nick as a friend, and to realize that he came from this— she couldn't decide if it made her like him more or less.

Nick came down the back stairs, a towel around his shoulders, dressed in a clean white T-shirt and jeans. He was drying his hair.

"I don't even want to know what you thought of

my house," Taj said, suddenly feeling painfully embarrassed at how proud she'd been of their back-yard view.

"What are you talking about? Your house is awe-some," Nick said, completely sincere.

"Okay, you don't have to lie to me—I've seen your house now," Taj joked, feeling relieved. Maybe it wasn't so bad that he'd seen the way she lived.

"Can I get you anything?" he asked.

"No, I'm good, thanks. Want a cookie?" she said, offering him a nut-brown cookie.

Nick began to shake his head—his stepmother had raised them to prefer wheat-free, carb-free organic snacks, but the sight of melted chocolate proved too tempting. "Sure," he said, picking it up.

"I loooove these," Taj said, licking chocolate off the side of her lip.

He was charmed. He'd only ever known girls who shrieked at the sight of an ice-cream cone and sub-sisted on dressing-free salad.

Taj removed a pint of milk from the bag as well. "Want a sip?" she asked, offering him her drink.

"No, thanks," he replied, holding up his trusty can of Red Bull.

"How can you drink that stuff? It's gross." Taj shuddered.

Nick looked at the can in his hand. It *was* gross. It was too sweet and sugary, and most of the time it gave him a headache. But somehow he couldn't help ordering it, buying it, drinking it. One day it was the only thing he would drink, the only thing his friends would drink. He tried to remember what he used to drink before reaching for the Red Bull, but he couldn't remember. "I like it," he said dubiously, putting down the can.

"Listen, Taj, I'm sorry about the other night. That was totally rude of me. Please tell your uncle I feel like an asshole."

"You were an asshole," Taj said. "But that's okay. You were upset about your sister."

"Friends?"

"Of course."

It was funny. They'd only known each other for what—a week? And already it felt so comfortable to be around him. She hadn't felt this way about a guy since—well, since Johnny. For a moment she felt guilty for a reason she didn't want to think about. She wasn't technically cheating on Johnny, after all. And besides, he was the one who had all those other girls.

Taj put down her cookie. She wiped her mouth carefully with a damp napkin. "I was thinking about what you said the other night, and I wanted to apologize. I know you thought I was being weird, so—"

He interrupted her. "I did some digging around. My friend Eric, who's a computer nerd, found some stuff. Did you know TAP is owned by Werner Music Group? You know, WMG?"

"You mean they bought it from YourPage."

"No, Eric said it's the opposite—they set up YourPage to back TAP."

"Really?" Taj asked, taking another cookie and not looking at him. "Huh. I always thought it was those two guys that started it—Mark and Jim . . . Jim's cute." Taj shrugged. "But for all we know they could be actors . . ."

"You know, Werner Music is one of the biggest labels around, if not the biggest," Nick said. Half the world's most popular music was distributed by the company. It had a finger in every musical pie—from hardcore rap to down-home country to everything in between.

"It's not Sutton Werner, is it? I heard his dad is some music mogul," Taj said innocently.

"Yeah, his dad's the biggest deal in the music industry. You know, his grandfather started the company. He discovered Jimi Hendrix, Janis Joplin . . . and his dad managed Jeff Buckley and Nirvana. Sutton grew up here, in L.A., the Palisades. His family moved to New York and he transferred to Bennet just this year. I heard he'd been kicked out of a couple schools—Choate, St. Lawrence, Harvard-Westlake. Anyway, I always thought he was a bit of a twerp. You?" he asked. "What do you know about Sutton?"

Taj slouched on the counter, breaking the cookie in half. "The same as everyone. Not much." She looked like she was going to evade the question again, but she kept talking. "Actually, he was Johnny's manager."

"No way. Sutton?'

"Yeah. He—he approached Johnny. When Johnny first put up his songs online, Sutton sent him an e-mail, telling him he could help him, you know, with his career and stuff. He was always very professional."

"And he throws those TAP parties. So it all goes back to him," Nick said.

"What do you mean?"

"I mean, everyone knows they're Sutton's parties, right?"

"I guess." Taj shrugged. "We didn't know that at first."

"We?"

"Johnny and me. But then when he asked Johnny to play several of the parties, we kind of figured out that he was behind the whole thing."

"How'd you guys meet anyway?"

"Me and Sutton?"

"No, you and Johnny," Nick asked.

"Online."

"Of course."

"It wasn't like that," Taj said, blushing. "I don't meet guys online. It's not my thing."

"Only in front of locked doors?" Nick asked, teasing.

"Right."

"So was Johnny some homeschooled genius? That's what TAP always said."

"Homeschooled? Johnny?" Taj laughed. "He's from Van Nuys. He went to Van Nuys High till he dropped out."

"Really. I always thought he was some kind of music savant."

"No—" Then Taj caught herself. "I mean, he was. But not that kind. He was pretty ordinary. He just played up that part—you know, Johnny Silver, artiste. Mr. Sensitive. But he was a pretty normal kid. Except when it came to music. Johnny was crazy about music."

"You think he's alive?"

"He's got to be. I mean, he's seventeen years old. You know? And famous. If he were dead, we'd hear about it, right?"

Nick nodded.

Taj took his hand. "What about your sister? Anything?"

Nick shook his head. "Nothing. I just wish she'd call. I'm sure she's fine. I mean, Fish is a pretty savvy kid. She can handle herself."

"I'm sure she'll turn up," Taj said, putting a hand on his shoulder. "I'm sure she's fine."

Nick

THE HUNTINGTON FAMILY BRUNCH AT THE IVY AT the Shore was a tradition that went back all the way to the mid-nineties, when his father first cracked the box office top ten with an action thriller. Since then, every family celebration—graduation, birthday, anniversary—was spent at the illustrious café. Huntington père preferred the more casual, laid-back Ivy in Santa Monica rather than the showier one in West Hollywood; as befitted a producer, he preferred to be behind the scenes rather than in front of the camera. Besides, no one would recognize him anyway, and he would be brushed aside in favor of one of the starlets he employed.

"Stars—they have no money," Nick's dad was fond of saying. His other favorite saying was "Stars—

they're employees," with a derision honed from more than a decade's worth of producing summer blockbusters, hiring and firing actors and actresses at will.

Nick's father was the picture of the L.A. mogul: tanned, fit, dressed casually in a white Polo shirt and scruffy jeans. His stepmother, Evelyn, was the polished California career woman at rest in her pastel Richard Tyler ensemble.

There was nothing to celebrate. Fish was technically still missing, although David and Evelyn didn't seem too concerned; they had somehow convinced themselves this was just another prank Fish was playing—another cry for attention—or perhaps they were in deep throes of denial. Nick couldn't decide. He took a sip of the overpriced lemonade and looked from one parent to the other warily.

"I fired Rosa this morning," Evelyn suddenly announced, after the waiter had taken their round of orders.

"Why?" Nick asked.

"She was stealing from me."

"Rosa?" Nick was aghast. The Guatemalan housekeeper had been with them for years. She was not only a trusted member of the family, but the children's main caretaker.

"I couldn't believe it either. But there was stuff

missing . . ." Evelyn shrugged. "Nothing too expensive, thank God. But pieces of jewelry. Money from my wallet. I would never have noticed except I needed cash to tip my hairdresser the other day, and I knew I had sixty dollars in my wallet, but it was gone. Anyway, who else would take it?"

Nick crinkled his brow. Something didn't add up. For the past few days, Citibank had left several messages for a "Pish Langley"—they were still trying to get a hold of Fish for some reason.

"That reminds me," his father said. "Has anyone seen my Patek Philippe? I had it out the other day and I can't seem to find it. It's very odd."

"No, haven't seen it," Nick said.

"Rosa. I'm telling you. You can never trust the help. Not even if they've been with you for twenty years. It's such a shame." Evelyn sighed. "The Patek that Nicole sent you for Christmas?"

"Yes." David grumbled. "Actors," he said in his usual dismissive tone. "Still. It's a twenty-thousand-dollar watch."

Nick suddenly realized he hadn't seen his own watch in a long time. Not to mention, small bills had been disappearing from his wallet every once in a while. He'd chalked it up to bad math on his part, but the other day he could have sworn he had a hundred-dollar bill in there, and it was just gone the next morning.

But he couldn't believe Rosa was responsible for any of it.

Suddenly he remembered how Fish always seemed to need money. She'd asked for a fifty before the party, and she'd been complaining for weeks before then about how she never got enough allowance. What would she need the money for? he wondered. She had everything she could ever want—neither David nor Evelyn was stingy in that direction. If anything, they erred in spoiling the kids too much. If she'd needed more money, she should have asked for a bigger allowance.

But maybe she couldn't ask for a bigger allowance, because she needed money fast, and soon. And maybe she'd needed more money than a raise in her allowance could provide. But for what?

"Can you imagine," Evelyn was saying. "A thief! In our house!" She shuddered.

Taj

THE NEXT DAY, AT THE STATION, TAJ GOT A PHONE call from Nick.

"Wanna hear Johnny's song again?" she asked.

"No, I'm not calling for a request."

"Oh," Taj said. She wasn't sure what he wanted, then.

"Listen, there's been all this weird stuff going on. I don't know why I'm telling you, but I feel like I have to tell somebody, and you seem to know a lot about this TAP stuff."

"I told you, I don't know anything about TAP. It was just some site where I met Johnny, that's all."

"Will you listen?"

"Of course," Taj said. "What's up?"

"There's been, like, a bunch of stuff missing from

the house." He told her about Evelyn's suspicions of Rosa, but how he couldn't believe it. "Little things, and some things only members of the family know about. I mean, could it be possible she's been sneaking back in the house and taking things?"

"Who? Fish?"

"Yeah. Is that weird? I mean, if she was home, why wouldn't she let us know?"

"What's been missing?"

"Oh, stuff, like my money clip and my dad's Patek Philippe."

Taj's ears pricked. Patek Philippe? She remembered Div talking about some insanely expensive watch Deck had received in the mail through TAP.

"Do you know any reason why a thirteen-year-old kid would need all this money?"

"Do you know about the gifting?" Taj asked before she could stop herself.

"The what?"

"Nothing," Taj said.

"C'mon, Taj. Spill it. Please. It's my sister I'm talking about here."

"All right," Taj said reluctantly. "There's this gifting thing—the wish lists—on TAP."

"What are you talking about?"

Taj told him. The rules, the hierarchy. How Div

and Deck received tons of gifts every week, how Johnny had been raking it in by the busload.

"But why would Fish . . . ," Nick said. Then the color drained from his face. His sister, the misfit, suddenly finding herself with a bunch of friends. He remembered one of Fish's new friends asking her if her "order" had come in; Fish had meekly asked her what her size was. Fish was buying friendship through TAP.

"Because she wanted to fit in, because she wanted to belong—that's why," Nick said, answering his own question. "And she was so insecure she would pay to be accepted."

"God," Taj said. She suddenly felt ill. She'd never thought of it that way, but of course that was what happened: The kids on the bottom, kids like Fish who didn't have enough friends to provide them with stuff, and who always had to kick up to their TAP "sponsors"— they would get behind, and getting behind meant humiliation on TAP. Then exorcism. Blackball.

"Taj, I need to ask you again. What goes on in that back room?" Nick said.

"You really want to know?"

"Yeah."

"You still think it has something to do with that? Because honestly, Nick, it doesn't."

"I just have to see for myself."

"Okay. There's another TAP party on Friday. I'll take you with me so you can see for yourself." *What could it hurt?* Taj thought. Maybe it could even be a little bit fun.

welcome to
TAP.COM

HOME   BROWSE   SEARCH   INVITE   FILM   MAIL   BLOG
FAVORITES   FORUM   GROUPS   EVENTS   VIDEO   MUSIC   CLASSIFIEDS

TAPPED IN....

Your news.
Your space.
Your funeral.
Put up
your stuff,
your videos,
your pics,
your photos,
your music.
Whateva
you gots for
us, we're
into it.

**MEMBERSHIP IS FREE.
RESPECT IS NOT.**

Member Login:

SCREEN NAME ☆

PASSWORD ☆

★ search TAP

YOU HAVE ONE NEW MESSAGE.

Displaying message:

EVENT INFORMATION
TAP PARTY
Call for location.
Back Room Rules Remain the Same.
No Word, No Entry.

★   [Click to Search for Friends] [Hot New People] [TAPPED IN Archives]   ★

Nick

FRIDAY NIGHT, JUST AS TAJ HAD PROMISED, WAS another TAP event. This one was in another empty mansion, this time in the Truesdale Estates. Taj told Nick she would meet him there, and he waited by the kitchen to see her.

There. Once again he was taken aback by how beautiful she was. She'd put her hair back in a low chignon, and her green eyes glittered in the dark light.

"Hey. Sorry I'm late. This place has, like, two kitchens, apparently," she said.

"No worries."

"So are you sure you're ready for this?"

"Yeah. I want to know."

"Okay, follow me. And remember, when they ask, it's Ambrose Bierce."

"*The Devil's Dictionary?*"

"Very good. I'm surprised you haven't been Tapped."

"What's that?"

"You'll see."

They made their way to the designated back-room area. The kid with the flashlight, this time one with a shaved head and a goatee, shone a light in their faces.

"What's the word?"

"Ambrose Bierce," they chorused.

They walked inside the dark room. "This is it? Nothing's happening," Nick whispered.

"Wait," Taj said. "Just wait, and be patient."

Someone handed them cups to drink. "TAP?" Nick asked.

"Yeah. Drink it. It makes it better."

"Okay," he said dubiously. It was only the second time he'd taken it. The sweet liquor hit him in the back of his throat and he began to feel woozy. A basket was being passed around. He watched as Taj reached in and grabbed something. Condoms.

The music—Johnny Silver's—was hypnotic and haunted. A light shone on a girl dancing in the middle of the room, with a needle.

A boy stepped forward.

Nick gasped as he watched the girl take the needle and start cutting him on his forearm.

"What the hell?"

"Shhhh," Taj said.

"What's going on?"

"He's just getting Tapped," she explained. "A tattoo. To show your allegiance to the divine Spirit."

"Spirit?"

"Can't you feel it?"

"No . . ."

Then he realized the room was stacked with pillows, and in the dark he could see bodies falling into them, and people disrobing. Was this for real? He looked to his side and noticed Taj was unzipping her top. She tossed it to the ground. Next she took off her blouse, then her bra.

She was dancing, sinuously, gracefully, and others were dancing with her. They were chanting. TAP kicked in, and he felt delirious from a feeling of infinite joy and ecstasy. He looked around, and thought he recognized a dark-haired girl slithering across the floor. Oh, yeah. It was Maxine. How funny was that. He gave her a smile, and she met his eye. There was a flash of surprise when she recognized him; then she turned away.

He pulled off his sweater and his shirt. Taj danced over to him. She was a goddess.

"Kiss me," she whispered.

"What's in this drink?" Nick slurred, feeling dizzy.

Taj lifted her chin up and Nick swayed on his feet, so they fell back into the pillows, together, skin to skin, mouth to mouth, feeling the heat of the room and the other bodies and letting the beat of the music pull them toward each other.

Nick laid his body on top of hers, put his hands on her chest, felt her damp skin sliding on his, and Taj twined her legs around his to pull him even closer. He put a hand on the zipper of her jeans and she guided it downward. They embraced.

Then there were other people around him, touching him, pulling them apart, and soon it wasn't just Taj he was kissing, but other girls. There were other hands, a million hands, all over his body, and he was falling back, back into the pillows, into the pile. *Disappear. Disappear. Disappear.*

He didn't know what he was doing, he didn't know why he was doing it, only that it felt good, it felt really good, and he hadn't felt this good in such a long time.

WHEN IT WAS OVER, TAJ EXPLAINED THE RITUAL over burgers at Mel's Diner, in a matter-of-fact fashion, as if they were discussing the weather.

"It's called the Initiation of the Spirit," Taj explained, taking a huge bite and stuffing a few french fries into her mouth. A night in the back room always made her hungry.

"Uh-huh," Nick said.

God, he was so shy and so cute about it. He was obviously embarrassed about what they had done in there, but there was nothing to be embarrassed about. That was the whole beauty of the ritual. It was about being free, about being liberated, about being yourself. It was a ritual that celebrated your body and the love it could bring, without emotional consequences. And they were always careful. It was the one place where you could be yourself.

That's why it was so addictive. It was so against everything they'd been taught—that hooking up was bad, that bodies were something to be ashamed of, that it was wrong to feel the way they felt. They were young and carefree, and the ritual celebrated this.

To be one with the Spirit was to commune with angels. This was the Angels' Practice.

Taj remembered the first time she realized she'd even fooled around with Deck during one of the rituals. But both of them had been cool about it, had joked about it, even. She loved Deck; she loved Johnny. In the back room, she loved everybody. Johnny had hooked up with Div in the back room, too. It didn't matter. It was all about sharing love in there.

At least, it was at first. That night, it was like the first time, innocent and sweet. Lately the back room had taken on a darker meaning, and she hadn't felt so comfortable. There were too many boys just standing around watching. It was creepy. But that night, with Nick, she'd felt safe.

"It's based on a pagan fertility ritual, a dance to celebrate the crops," Taj said. "I think someone in TAP read too much Marion Zimmer Bradley and decided they wanted to try it on their own."

Nick nodded. "Who's that?"

"Some author, wrote a bunch of goddess-themed novels. Good trashy stuff."

"And you buy it? The whole Spirit thing?"

Taj took a handful of fries and chewed on them before answering. She thought about his question. "I guess I didn't at first, but then I took TAP, and it enhances it. Makes it . . . I don't know . . . dreamy somehow. It's like a really good dream, the back room. It's not real."

Nick still couldn't look at her.

"C'mon, I told you it wasn't anything bad. Your sister . . . she's a little young for it, but no one is forced to do anything. It's free will; you only go so far as you're comfortable with. And maybe she was just there to watch the Tapping."

"The cutting?"

"Yeah. The tattoos. The angel wings."

"What's up with that?"

"Oh, it just means you're part of it for real. You're supposed to pledge your allegiance to TAP for a million years. It's kind of silly, really. But there's no harm."

Nick's face blanched. He'd seen that tattoo on Fish's arm. Was that what it meant?

"C'mon, Nick, now that you've seen what it is, you have to agree there's nothing wrong with it. I mean,

TAP didn't exactly invent free love, did they? I mean, it's been around before. This is just the latest version. They used to call us hippies. Now they call us hipsters," she joked.

She wondered if she had been right in taking him to the back room. But it was too late now.

Nick

ON MONDAY THE FOLLOWING WEEK NICK STILL couldn't get over what had gone down in the back room. Taj was acting like it was nothing, like it was something she did all the time, with anybody. But to him it felt different. Eric wasn't at school that day, and his buddy wasn't picking up his phone, either. He wanted to ask Eric if he'd experienced the same thing in the back room. Oh, well.

Nick saw Maxine at the cafeteria—and an image from the ritual, unbidden, came to his mind. How long had she been participating? Was that where she first hooked up with Sutton? he wondered.

He went through the motions of school—AP classes, lunch, more AP classes, college-counselor session, then soccer practice, and he was done.

The school parking lot was almost empty when Nick came out of the locker room. He zapped his keys at his car and got inside. As he drove off, he noticed a black Escalade with tinted windows pull out from across the street. It looked similar to the one he had seen earlier that morning, tailing him down the canyon on the way to school.

Nick thought nothing of it. Tons of people in L.A. drove black Escalades. You couldn't go down Beverly without seeing at least two. He drove up to Mulholland. It had gotten dark early, and the street was winding and curvy.

There was a sharp curve on the road, and Nick slowed down, only to notice a black Escalade bearing down on his right.

"What the fuck," Nick muttered, trying to shake the car off his tail.

But the lumbering SUV powered up, and Nick turned the wheel one hundred eighty degrees to get out of the way, spinning the convertible into the ditch. The car rolled over, bouncing Nick against the ceiling and shattering his right cheek into the glass, and he passed out into blackness.

When Nick woke up, a paramedic was shining a light into his eyes.

Melissa de la Cruz

A FEW DAYS AFTER SHE HAD TAKEN NICK TO THE
TAP party, Taj geared up in a Santa Monica school
yard for the qualifying rounds for the Vancouver
tournament, one of the most respected annual
skateboarding contests. Even the pros attended.
Only those who made it to the final rounds at the
regional level made it to Canada, glory, and skater
history.

Div and Deck were already there.

"Check it out—we got sponsors!" Div said, holding aloft a new board decked out with dozens of stickers for Lost Angeles, an up-and-coming skateboard
company based in Venice Beach.

"Big pimpin'." Deck grinned, pointing to his Lost
Angeles logo T-shirt.

"Nice." Taj smiled.

"If we get flicked in a magazine, we get five hundred cash. Plus, each sticker in the photo is fifty bucks. Twelve stickers is six hundred bucks, even if it's in the same photo," Div explained proudly.

"And if we make it through, they'll pay to send us to Vancouver, maybe even Tampa," Deck added, meaning the biggest tournament there was— Tampa was the mother lode. Mount Everest. Even if you didn't place at Tampa, just the fact that you were there was enough to send your hits skyrocketing.

"So what else did they send?" Taj asked. She'd heard about the sponsor packages—large cardboard boxes that came with tons of loot.

"A coupla boards, some shoes, T-shirts. But Deck's already sold half of his for drinks and smokes." Div smirked.

"Typical."

Taj squinted against the sun, waiting for her turn while her friends lined up by the half-pipe. They were wearing their matching Lost Angeles T-shirts, and the logo was all over their shorts, their shoes, even their socks. Not to mention screaming out of their boards. For their sake, Taj hoped they got shot for something. They looked like walking bill-boards.

Most skaters didn't even care about the checks—the cash prizes that came with third, second, and first place. It was about footage—kids and adults watched videos millions of times online, traded the most popular ones, studied them for moves. It was about infamy, admiration, a certain kind of fame.

Sure, some skaters ended up with MTV shows or their own Xbox video, but most kids simply craved the respect of their peers rather than a taste of the limelight. Choice video footage of Taj doing a half-cab off a nine-set that Deck had shot in a secret spot off Manhattan Beach had been accessed on TAP more times than the latest Tony Hawk video.

Div flubbed her aerial, and Deck fell down hard on a full-pipe loop, but Taj rolled down, feeling good, feeling the adrenaline high. Now she had to just set up for the jump—but at a sharp turn the wheels suddenly locked, tipping her head over feet down the ramp, crashing down into the concrete. There was a gasp from the crowd, and when Taj opened her eyes, she was confused as to what she was doing on the ground.

"Are you hurt? Don't move!" a med tech advised, checking Taj's pulse.

"I think I'm okay," Taj said, gingerly lifting herself up. She waved to the crowd to indicate she was all right, and limped off the course. She was bleeding from both knees and her elbows, and there was a gash on the side of her head.

"Oh my god, Taj, are you okay?" Div asked, rolling over. "What happened?"

"Dude, that was one wipeout," Deck marveled.

Taj picked up her board and checked the wheelbase. "I'm not sure—I think the wheels locked," she said, turning it over. "Wait a minute—these aren't my wheels."

"Are you sure?" Deck asked.

"Yeah, look. I just got new wheels put in, and look, these are already concave. And the wheels I got were red—these are black."

"Are you saying someone changed them?" Div asked incredulously. "Just to fuck up a competitor?"

"I don't know," Taj said, holding the side of her head and still feeling dizzy. But somehow she didn't think the faulty gear was due to a skater having a Tonya Harding moment.

She went to the bathroom to clean up the wound, and opened her backpack.

Melissa de la Cruz

Inside was a note.

YOU BROKE THE RULES. WE BREAK YOU.
THIS IS YOUR FIRST WARNING

Fuck! Why had she brought Nick to the ritual? What had gotten into her? Now she was really in trouble.

THE ACCIDENT HAD BEEN SCARY, BUT NOT SERIOUS.
He'd spent a few hours in the hospital for observa-
tion. Rosa had checked him out, since she was the
emergency contact on his insurance. Still acting as
substitute mom even though the family had fired her.
Their former housekeeper weepily declared her inno-
cence, and Nick assured her that he, for one, didn't
believe a word of the accusation.

When he got home that evening, he logged in to
TAP to ask Eric if he could help him figure out something. Eric hadn't been at school all week. There was
a mono bug going around, and Nick had assumed
his friend had caught it. But Eric wasn't logged in all
day or all night, and when Nick went to his page, he
realized the last time Eric had logged in was the

same night he'd sent Nick all that information about how the Werner Music conglomerate owned TAP.

That was unsettling. Eric was *always* online. He was obsessed with checking his e-mail and comments. Nick sent him an e-mail, telling him to get in touch as soon as he received it.

But several days went by, and whenever Nick checked, Eric's page still wasn't updated, and his last login time was the same. Now Nick was truly worried. Was Eric really sick? Had they gotten to Eric, too? It just wasn't like Eric to suddenly be so hard to get a hold of. No one was picking up his cell phone, and when Nick called Eric's house, their housekeeper told him Eric's parents were in the Bahamas. If Eric was gone, no one would even notice.

He decided he would go visit Taj at the station. Ask her again what she knew about TAP. Besides, after what happened the other night at the ritual, he really wanted to see her again.

She opened the door to the station and the first thing he noticed was an ugly gash on her forehead and a purple bruise on the side of her cheek.

"*Hola*," she said cheerfully, as if she didn't look like she'd just survived a beating. Her eyes widened when she saw him as well.

His head was bandaged, and his arm was in a sling. He had broken capillaries around his eyes.

They stared at each other.

"Skateboard accident!"

"Car crash!"

"It looks worse than it is," Taj assured. "How about you? Are you okay?"

Nick nodded. "Nothing serious. They thought I'd have a concussion, and the car's a wreck, but I got lucky. Just a couple of bumps and cuts."

"Me too." Taj told him about the faulty gear on her skateboard, and she looked like she was about to say something more, but she didn't. That habit of hers was getting on his nerves.

Nick frowned and told her about the black Escalade running him off the road up on Mulholland Drive. "I thought it was just some asshole driver. Trying to drive and text on a BlackBerry at the same time. But now I think it might have been deliberate. I think it was following me around, you know, after you took me to that ritual thing."

"Be serious. Why would the ritual lead to something like this?" Taj asked, although she looked nervous.

"I don't know, Taj, why don't you tell me?"

"What's that supposed to mean?"

"Did you really have a skateboard accident? I've

seen you on your board. I can't imagine you falling off that thing."

Taj blushed. "It was an accident."

"I just don't want to see you get hurt," Nick said.

Taj's face softened. "I can take care of myself."

The tension in the room abated somewhat, and Nick decided he would drop it since Taj wasn't being more forthcoming right then.

"So, this is where the magic happens." He sighed.

"The *Manic* happens," Taj corrected, showing him where he could sit across from her while she ran the show. "Although I have no idea why Johnny called it the *Manic Hour*. He played the most mellow music."

"A sarcastic man," Nick said, looking through the CD stacks. "What are these?" he asked, picking up what looked like an eight-track cassette tape.

"Oh, they're PSAs—public service announcements. We're a government-funded station, so we have to run them every half hour."

"Funny."

"Isn't it? Usually what happens is kids play the anti-drug ones and then right after play 'Stairway to Heaven' or something. You know, that kind of thing. I'll cue up one that Johnny always played. It's from the wood council or some sort of agricultural government office."

The song ended, and Taj inserted the cassette. A voice intoned, "I'd like to discuss the many benefits of using *hardwood* to build your family's home. Hardwood is very easy to get! Hardwood is very easy to keep! Hardwood is your only choice!"

"I remember that. Hilarious," Nick said, taking a seat and laughing. "I brought some drinks—want one?" he asked, holding up a carton of milk.

She accepted it with a smile, and he could tell she was pleased that he'd remembered her favorite drink.

Nick looked over Taj's shoulder to the computer screen, and she felt a prickle on her skin as she felt his breath on her cheek. "What are you looking for?" he asked. He wondered if he should mention Eric's disappearance. Although when you looked at it, it was absurd to think some website was behind it. Maybe Eric had gone out of the country with his parents. They did that sometimes, just took the kids away without telling the school or letting anybody know, and for the most trivial reasons, like when they'd rented Mick Jagger's villa for the week at a cheap price.

"Nothing," she said.

They drank for a while in silence. Once in a

while Taj would let Nick listen to the music on the headphones so he could hear what she was playing.

"So this is what other kids do," Nick mused, handing them back.

"What do you mean?"

"I mean, it's Friday night, and usually I'm like stupid drunk by this time, bumming around somewhere," he said ruefully. "Course, probably not tonight, since I'm on so much medication."

"Are you bored?" Taj asked, feeling a little offended.

"No, not at all," Nick replied, rumpling his hair and leaning back on his chair so it tilted backward on an angle. "This is actually really nice. It's fun, in a different way."

Taj appraised him silently. "Johnny and I used to spend Friday night just like this. He'd play the songs, and I'd sit where you're sitting right now. It was the best time of my life," she said matter-of-factly, turning away to put a new song on the radio.

"Even before TAP? The ritual?"

Taj blushed.

"Listen—I know you're not supposed to talk about it, but I think we should."

"Talk about what?" Taj asked.

"What happened in the back room."

"What happened?" Taj asked, her voice light.

"You and me . . . we . . ."

"We?"

"Hooked up, I guess." It was strange to be the guy who wanted to talk; it was usually the other way around.

"So?"

"What do you mean, so?"

"I mean, it's just part of the ritual. It doesn't mean anything," Taj said, not meeting his eyes.

"Well, I disagree, because it certainly meant something to me."

"Really," Taj whispered.

Nick stood behind the chair, and leaned down again so that his cheek was against hers. "Yeah. It meant a lot."

"You're just . . ."

"What?" Nick asked. He turned her toward him, and he could see she was trembling.

"Kiss me," he said. "Here. Now. Without some stupid drink to make you feel like you can dismiss it as nothing. Without some stupid crowd and some back room and password or whatever. Kiss me."

Taj's eyes teared up. "I can't."

"You guys have been brainwashed into thinking this thing is good for you, that this thing is right. But

it's not. Love isn't free, Taj. And it's not about everyone. It's about you and me. Here, right now. *Kiss me.*"

She turned to him, and finally it was Nick who
kissed her, and he pulled her down to the floor so that
the two of th   roved around behind the big desk,
     sed her some more, and he looked into her
eyes, and she nodded, and he helped her out of her
T-shirt, out of her jeans, and it was just the two of
them, together, with the lights on, and Johnny's song
playing in the background, on an endless loop, so
that kids that evening would think Taj was on some
kind of kick.

Nick kissed her and kissed her until it felt like his
lips would burn from all the kisses.

And this was good. He was right. This was the
way it should be. Not in the dark. Not with strangers.
Just the two of them.

Together.

Resurrection

*"angelheaded hipsters burning
for the ancient heavenly connection . . ."*
—ALLEN GINSBERG, *"HOWL"*

HOME · BROWSE · SEARCH · INVITE · FILM · MAIL · BLOG
FAVORITES · FORUM · GROUPS · EVENTS · VIDEO · MUSIC · CLASSIFIEDS

TAPPED IN....

Your news.
Your space.
Your funeral.
Put up
your stuff,
your videos,
your pics,
your photos,
your music.
Whateva
you gots for
us, we're
into it.

MEMBERSHIP IS FREE.
RESPECT IS NOT.

Member Login:

SCREEN NAME☆

PASSWORD☆

search TAP

!!!!!New Event Invitation!!!!

Sutton Productions presents

EXCLUSIVE ENGAGEMENT

Johnny Silver

Returns

8:00 pm

The Hollywood Bowl

Tickets On Sale Tomorrow!

The Triumphant Concert!

This event is for TAP
members only
[RSVP Now]
The guest list is kept private

★ [Click to Search for Friends] [Hot New People] [TAPPED IN Archives] ★

NOW SHE'D DONE IT. NOW IT WAS REALLY complicated. She hadn't been looking for a boyfriend, but what could she do about it? He was just so sweet. She should have been stronger. That wasn't the way it was supposed to go down. She was only supposed to find out how much he knew, and maybe lead him on a little. But now things were out of control.

The call had come in that morning. She had been expecting it ever since the ritual. Time to face the music.

Those new to L.A. always missed the entrance to the Chateau Marmont; the first time she and Johnny had visited, they had driven all the way past it and had to backtrack. The hotel was located on a hidden curved street off Sunset Boulevard. They'd felt like two rubes.

The hotel lobby was a study in eclectic baronial

splendor, with deep walnut paneling, deep-seated antique couches, and George Nelson lamps. As she walked in, the concierge greeted her. In the months when she and Johnny had lived at the Chateau, they had gotten friendly.

"Miss Holder, I trust lunch was to Mr. Silver's satisfaction?" The clerk beamed. "I did have the chef prepare it according to his request."

"Johnny?"

That was totally odd.

A woman in a sports bra and leggings, holding a yapping poodle on a leash, was leaving the hotel just as she walked in.

"Hi, Taj. Glad to see you and Johnny are back."

Back?

She walked quickly through the pool area, where several people were suntanning. They looked up at her and began to wave madly.

"Taj!"

"Johnny's looking good!"

"Tell him we say hi!"

Taj nodded to them, feeling more confused than ever as she ducked into the tower elevator and hit the button. The two-bedroom penthouse took up the entire top floor. With a beating heart, Taj took the elevator up.

The door was open, so she pushed it in.

There were voices coming from inside the room.

Johnny?

Oh my God, is Johnny really back? Her heart beat in excitement. *Was Sutton telling the truth?*

A figure stepped out into the hallway.

"Taj. Took you long enough to get here." It was Sutton, in a white Chateau Marmont bathrobe. "Come on in."

Taj followed him inside. The penthouse was a sprawling space, decorated in a modern-gothic vibe— gray velvet couches, Plexiglas lamps—with a panoramic view of Los Angeles from the ocean all the way to downtown. There were guitars and pieces of clothing strewn about, and the remnants of a large party were in evidence—empty beer and wine bottles, spills on the white rug. Taj thought she could even see a bunch of bodies passed out in the back hallways that led to the bathrooms.

Sutton led her to the outdoor patio. He pulled a crumpled cigarette pack from his back pocket and offered one to Taj.

Taj shook her head, and Sutton shrugged. He lit the crooked cigarette with a lighter from the coffee table and took a long puff.

"What's going on? Where's Johnny? Is he here?"

"All in good time."

"What the fuck do you mean by that, Sutton?"

"I mean, be patient and all will be revealed."

"Where's Johnny?"

"God, you are a broken record."

Taj crossed her arms and frowned.

"Hey, you want anything? Red Bull? Vodka?"

Taj shook her head.

"Looks like you got a bad cut there," Sutton said. "Does it hurt?"

"No . . ."

"Pity about the wheels on your board. You should really be more careful next time," Sutton said.

It was just as she'd thought.

"That was low, Sutton. I could really have hurt myself, you know."

"It was just a warning."

"For what?" she asked belligerently, although she already knew the reasons.

"You know very well he didn't have the password, Taj. He sullied the ritual. You brought in an unTapped player. It's against the rules. You really put me in an awkward position there. How can the back room be exclusive if just anyone can get in? I had to do something about it. A member complained."

"I didn't think there were any rules," Taj said. "Isn't that what you told us the first time? That there are no rules, no prophets, no pamphlets. It's not a religion; there are no magicians, no preachers, no salesmen. That we can make it up as we go along."

"Well, rules change." Sutton smiled.

"Nick's accident—that was you, too, wasn't it?"

"It's not my fault he's a bad driver," Sutton said, shrugging.

"Where's Johnny? You said you'd found him. Am I going to get to see him? Is he all right? What do you want, Sutton?"

"What I've always wanted, Taj. *You*." Sutton smiled. Taj could see a row of crooked teeth, all yellow. It was the smile of the devil.

Nick

THAT MORNING, NICK NOTICED THE MAILBOX door was hanging off its hinge. Ever since Evelyn had fired Rosa, nothing was the same in the house. The new housekeeper forgot to leave weekday meals, let alone sort through the mail. He collected the letters and took them inside.

Cable bills, electric bills, unsolicited mail for his dad from enterprising film students who had found his home address, catalogs from Neiman Marcus and Barneys, a museum calendar, assorted charity invitations, voting pamphlets. Most of it junk. He sorted the mail according to family member and noticed several thick white envelopes addressed to his stepsister. An envelope from MasterCard. Another from Capital One. Another from AmEx.

They were credit card bills. But as far as Nick knew, Fish didn't have credit cards—her mom wouldn't allow it. Besides, who would give a thirteen-year-old a credit card? Wasn't that against the law?

Then something else caught his eye.

A postcard, addressed to him. With a message scrawled on the back.

She's not who you think she is. Follow the stars.

It was a postcard of the San Fernando Valley, a wide nighttime shot of a residential neighborhood lit by streetlights. There was a stamp and a post-mark, and the return address was for a house in Van Nuys.

Nick decided he would have to investigate.

He drove up the 405 and took the Van Nuys Boulevard exit. It was just over the hill from Bel-Air, mere minutes away, and yet it might as well have been in the middle of north Jersey. Where Nick lived, one block down from Mulholland was the Valley, while one block up was Bel-Air. Yet the difference in bragging rights, real-estate prices, and status conferred was immeasurable. In some circles having an 818 area code was tantamount to social suicide.

The address was in one of the older developments—a succession of shabby one-level tract houses that were impossible to tell apart. Nick parked his dad's Mercedes in the driveway.

"Yes." The door was opened a crack.

"I . . ." Nick wasn't quite sure why he was there. But before he could explain, or think of an excuse, the door opened.

"Oh. Yeah. He said you'd stop by," the woman said.

He?

"His room's over there."

What room?

Nick walked inside the house. The carpet was beige, the couches were beige, and there was very little art or any sign of personality in the décor—it was standard JCPenney catalog furniture, with the occasional Target end table thrown in.

"Second one to the right," she directed. This must be Johnny's mother; Taj's description of her was accurate. She looked haggard and exhausted, and shuffled rather than walked.

He found the room. It was small, about the size of a jail cell, the walls painted crudely with black and silver paint. There were books everywhere, guitar magazines, and instruments of every variety, from six-foot-tall amps to a stand-up bass. He noticed something tacked on the closet door—a picture of the MiSTakes, inscribed with the words *For Johnny—don't we look great? Love, Taj*. With a start, he realized he was in Johnny Silver's room. Taj was telling the truth. He was just some kid from the Valley. Everything was so ordinary. Ordinary and cheap.

Nick drew in a long breath and sat down at Johnny's old desk. What exactly was he looking for? Why had he received the postcard? He opened the desk drawer. Pens, pencils, sketchbooks, music sheets, paper clips, old copies of music magazines—*Wire*, *Magnet*, *Alternative Press*. Nick was systematic and efficient. He looked under the bed and unearthed Johnny's old guitar cases from the closet. He went through every niche, cranny, and possible hiding place. But he found nothing.

His phone rang. Taj. "Where are you?" she asked.

"Out," he said. He hadn't told her about the postcard yet. *She's not who you think she is.* The writer was obviously talking about Taj. Not that Nick put any stock in anonymous notes. "You?"

"I'm with a friend," she said. She sounded tired, almost defeated. He thought of the other night. The two of them, alone in the station. The feel of her skin, the smell of her hair, the softness of her lips. They'd been hooking up almost every day since it happened. Nick sneaking into her bedroom in the flats, or having her up in Bel-Air on the weekend when no one was home. The two of them running around the giant empty house wearing nothing but their underwear. "Call me when you get back?" she whispered.

"Of course."

After a few hours of futile searching, he yawned and lay down on Johnny's bed. He looked up at the ceiling, hung with glow-in-the-dark stars that Johnny must have put up when he was a little kid and had never taken down. He picked up the postcard, glancing at the bright little house glowing under similar faint stars. Something on the ceiling caught his eye. A miniscule jagged edge.

Could it be?

Nick stood up on the bed, reached over, and tapped on it. Nothing. He pushed in, but nothing gave. Finally he slammed his fist against it in frustration. And the crack jogged. Nick gasped and lifted the wood. His arms flailed about the ceiling's crawl space, searching . . . and then his fingers touched something.

Taj

TAJ QUICKLY HUNG UP THE PHONE WHEN SUTTON came back onto the terrace. "I want you to meet someone," he said.

A boy walked behind him.

At first, Taj was convinced Johnny had come back. But then she realized it was only a trick of the light, a trick of the eye. But it was a very, very good trick indeed.

The boy standing in front of them had Johnny's brilliant platinum hair, although if you squinted you could see the dark roots on his crown. And Taj would bet that his violet eyes were due to contacts. Still, the boy had the same thin build, the same aristocratic nose, the same scrawny hips that looked good in a pair of low-rise Levi's.

This wasn't Johnny. This was a reproduction. A copy. A clone. What was Sutton doing?

"Who are you?"

"Me?" The boy looked at Sutton. "I'm not sure."

"Leave us." Sutton dismissed him.

"You said Johnny was here."

"He was. He is. I don't know where he went. He really was here, just a minute ago." Sutton giggled. "Oh, Taj, you're too funny."

"Where is he?"

"You just saw him. With your own two eyes. If that's not Johnny, I don't know who is," Sutton said. "Impressive, isn't it? Only very few people are going to be able to tell the difference. I found him through TAP, of course. One of Johnny's most ardent fans. And the thing is, he really believes he's Johnny. It's fantastic."

"You're not thinking of . . ."

"Oh, yes."

"You're not serious."

"I'm nothing but serious," Sutton said. "Haven't you checked your in-box? Tickets go on sale next week. I suggest you buy them now. The comeback concert of the decade. The missing rock star rising like a phoenix from the ashes."

"You knew this would happen," Taj whispered.

"Supernova. You knew what would happen to Johnny. You *planned* this."

"I guessed," Sutton said. "I didn't know. There's a difference."

"Bastard. You pushed him too hard."

"Me? I didn't do anything. Not like you, Taj. Not like you."

"I'm leaving."

"You used him too, Taj."

"Not like that. Not the way you did. This is sick, Sutton. He's a human being. But I want to know—why? Why the disappearance? Why the return?"

"If Elvis came back tomorrow, don't you think tickets would get sold out in an instant? You know there are people out there who still believe the King is alive. And his estate makes more money now that he's gone. It got me thinking, what if we created that phenomenon? The missing rock star—Kurt Cobain—coming back from the grave. Wouldn't it be delicious? And lucrative?"

"This is all about money. That's all it is."

"Taj, you make it sound so dirty."

"But why?"

"Johnny Silver is more of an idea than a real person," Sutton said. "People just need to believe in icons. Rock stars aren't real. They're beyond real.

Almost a figment of the imagination. If you remember, Johnny Silver isn't even his real name. Johnny Silver is an illusion. A mirage. Which means he can be replaced."

Taj gritted her teeth. Sutton had a point. Johnny Silver had been born John Smith.

Nick

IT WAS A BOX.

It was an old shoe box, and Nick carried it down from the ceiling with care. The lid was taped shut with several layers of packing tape, and Nick had to rip it open with a fingernail—a hard task since he bit his nails down to the quick. The tape made an angry sound as he unwound it from the box.

There's nothing in here, Nick thought. *Probably a bunch of kid stuff.* Johnny Silver's old secret hiding place. He wasn't sure what he was going to find—a diary? Notes? Plane tickets? Or nothing at all? A bunch of rocks?

He took a deep breath and lifted the lid.

• • •

Nick called Taj and asked her to meet him at the Beverly Center. It seemed an innocuous place; plus, Taj had voiced a hankering for more of those chocolate chip cookies. When she arrived, he told her about the mysterious postcard but not what was written on it. Told her how he'd traveled to Van Nuys. How he'd been inside Johnny's own house, and how the woman at the door seemed to be expecting him. Then he showed her what he'd found inside the box.

It was a notebook. With Johnny's name scrawled on the front.

"Where did you get that?" Taj asked, looking alarmed.

"I found it in the ceiling. Hidden, in a box."

She started paging through it. It was the kind of scrapbook that every angsty high school kid kept, full of doodles and profound statements that were actually lyrics from popular rock songs. *You got me blowin', blowin' my mind. Is it tomorrow, or just the end of time?*—Jimi Hendrix, "Purple Haze." *I'm so happy 'cause today I found my friends. They're in my head.*—Nirvana, "Lithium." There were sketches of Taj sitting moodily on a bed, a profile of Johnny with a guitar, and pages and pages of what looked like the full lyrics to several of Johnny's songs—"Secret Chord," "Alternate Reality," "What Is My Mind"—with many scratches and corrections. She put it down, looking a bit relieved, he noticed.

"Why would anyone want me to find Johnny Silver's notebook?" he asked.

Taj looked pensive. "Nick, I have to tell you something. This isn't Johnny's notebook."

"What do you mean? It's got his name on the front."

"I know. I put it there."

"What are you talking about?"

"I mean . . ." Taj shifted on her feet and looked anxious. "No one was ever supposed to know. But I wrote the songs. Johnny's songs, I mean. All of them. The journal is mine."

"Excuse me?" he asked.

"I know it looks bad, okay. That's why I didn't say anything before."

"What are you pulling here? Did you send me the postcard? What kind of game are you and Johnny playing, anyway? I thought you said he was a musical genius."

"I guess I should start from the beginning," she said quietly, twisting the edge of her shirt with her hands. "We met online. I told you that, right?"

Nick nodded.

"He sent me an e-mail promoting his show. I don't

think anyone even listened to it that much back then;
it was before the whole TAP thing really took off. But
I found it, and I liked what he was doing. Then I started calling him during the show. I would suggest a
couple of songs, even. A lot of songs. He seemed to
know what he wanted to play, but Johnny actually
didn't know a lot about music."

"Go on."

"But he was really interested to learn, so I told
him everything that I knew, bands that I liked,
singer-songwriters that I loved. We talked and talked
and talked, late into the night, and it was nice because
I had a friend . . . I mean, I have friends, but not like
Johnny was. Deck and Div—they're not interested so
much in music. Sometimes I think all they have on the
brain are skateboards. But not me. I mean, it's fun and
all, but I don't want to go pro or anything. I mean, be
serious."

Taj nibbled on a cuticle on her thumb.

"So you told Johnny what to play . . . what bands,
what songs . . . ," Nick prodded.

"Yeah, I'd e-mail him playlists, suggestions, tell
him about the history of stuff. I don't know, I was kind
of running the whole show. Then the ratings started
going up, and he got picked up on TAP. It started getting huge. We DJed together as the MiSTakes."

She sighed. "What you have to understand about Johnny is that more than anything he wanted to be a musician, to be famous. He showed me what he'd written—but it was awful. I felt bad for him. So I showed him the stuff I was working on." She sighed.

"And he would sing it, and it was really good. So he released that demo—you know, the one everyone downloaded? And then it got even bigger, and then there was all that buzz when he played at that party, and then Sutton came along, and record companies started calling, and they wanted an album, so I worked on a couple of songs for him. All right. I worked on all the songs."

"You did all that? And you never wanted anything for yourself? Credit, at least?"

"Don't you see? It would have ruined it. What if all those kids, all those fans, knew that Johnny didn't write his own songs? He'd be laughed at. Look at Kurt Cobain—even his friggin' journals are best-sellers. Jim Morrison. Jimi Hendrix. If you don't write your own songs, you might as well be Britney Spears. And just between you and me, even she writes her own songs.

"Anyway, I didn't really want anything. I just wanted him. Johnny. I loved him, even if it felt like he was only with me because of the music, because of the songs I wrote. I didn't care. At least we were together.

"But I was getting nervous. It was kind of fun for a while, to pretend, to have created this thing, this 'Johnny Silver' dude. It was a game. It wasn't real. But then people started calling him the new Bob Dylan. *Rolling Stone* was shooting him for the cover. I told him we had to stop. We couldn't be part of this fraud that Sutton was spinning. I told him if he kept going, he'd be some kind of false idol. But he wouldn't listen. He was addicted to it by then—the attention, the money. I told him I was quitting. I didn't want to do it anymore. I didn't want to be part of it. Kids were, like, going crazy thinking he was this genius or something. They wanted nothing more than to be like him, to be him. It was getting scary."

"So he booked," Nick said. "The night of the Viper."

"Yeah. I guess. I don't know what happened. I felt bad. Maybe I was too harsh on him. It's why I kept the show going—I was trying to tell him that wherever he is, it's okay. I forgive him. He can come back; it'll be all right. I'm not angry. Whatever happens . . . I mean, it's not like it's so bad to sing someone else's songs, right? That Jeff Buckley song he always played on his show—'Hallelujah'? Buckley didn't write it. It's a cover. Johnny never even knew that. He thought that song was so great, I didn't have the heart to tell him."

"Taj."

"Yeah?"

"What about the postcard?"

"I have no idea who sent you the postcard, or why."

She was lying. He had found other things in the notebook. He'd ripped them out before showing her. Pages and pages of notes: "Wish List Requirements"; "Angel-X?"; "Angels' Practice: a Manifesto." Odd scribbles of pronouncements—"Allegiance is required"; "Membership is final"—and weird recipes, as well as notes that looked like incantations, and rules. "Goddess Worship." "Scheduling." "Phenomena." "Experiments." None of it made any sense. And if it was her notebook, were they her notes, too?

She isn't who you think she is.

Nick drove off the parking lot and into traffic. "This is fine for me, thanks," Taj said when they reached the fringes of West Hollywood. "I can skate home from here." She hopped out of the car and shouldered her backpack and skateboard.

"Sure?"

"Yeah, I feel like being outside anyway." She

paused. "Hey, Johnny was a good guy. He didn't do anything wrong, you know? He just wanted to be a star. Don't think too badly of him, okay?" she asked. She probably meant, *Don't think too badly of me.*

IT HAD BEEN A RELIEF TO FINALLY ADMIT THEIR
secret to someone else. She'd been holding that
information inside for so long, she hardly believed it
was true. Maybe she was just dreaming it; maybe
Johnny *had* written all those songs. But seeing her
old composition notebook again brought it all back to
her.

All those nights sitting alone, listening, writing,
dreaming, doodling . . . the words coming out of a
dark secret place.

She hoped Nick wouldn't judge Johnny too harshly.
They had only been doing what seemed best, for both
of them. Johnny had wanted it so much, and she had
loved him so much she wanted him to get everything
he wanted.

The way it started had been so innocent. She had shown him her lyrics, and he'd played a few chords on the guitar. She'd suggested different ones, ones that worked better.

Then they'd recorded a few songs with his computer. Scratchy, Velvet Undergound–type lo-fi technology. It sounded awful, really, but they'd put it up on the site, under the name Johnny Silver. Johnny had posed for it, and they'd made up the whole background for him: the homeschooled rumor, the weird fetishes—they'd made him up. Johnny Silver didn't exist, really. He was their creation. It was a costume, like the skinny suits Johnny wore. Although the hair and the eyes were real enough.

They'd tried it first with the MiSTakes, but the four-way group didn't catch on like Johnny Silver did.

They'd never meant for it to get this far. But Sutton, he'd forced them—no, Taj thought, they'd been willing accomplices. Sutton knew everything. That Taj wrote the songs and Johnny sang them. Knew their secret all along.

And he'd shown them the workings of TAP. Thank God Nick hadn't found all the other stuff that was in there. The stuff they'd been working on. She had to tell Sutton it was over; they had to stop it now. They'd gone too far. The missing kids. Johnny's disappearance. It was getting way too freaky. That's not what she had wanted when she'd volunteered to help with the project.

But the roller coaster had already taken off, and she was strapped in her seat. She only hoped she could get off before it plunged over the cliff.

Melissa de la Cruz

Nick

THE CALL CAME WHEN NICK LEAST EXPECTED IT. THE
conversation with Taj was still bothering him. He was
wondering if he should confront her with the other
things he'd found. His head was swimming. He didn't
know what to think. But if she was so involved with
Johnny, what was her relationship to TAP? Wasn't
TAP just a front to sell Johnny's records, then? What was
her relationship to Sutton? And what did a made-up rock
star have to do with those weird Friday night parties in
the back room? How did it all tie in together? And the
wish list rule—what was that all about? All these
questions buzzed in his brain.

The voice on the phone was calm. "Is this Mr.
Nick Huntington?"

"Yes."

"We've got your sister here. Says she wants to come home."

Fish was in the hospital in Altadena, a half hour away from the city in the San Gabriel Valley. How had she ended up there? When Nick arrived, he was shocked to see how pale she looked, and how thin. The hospital explained that someone had dropped her off there that morning, leaving without identifying themselves. They'd found his number on her cell phone.

David and Evelyn were flying home. "Of course she's fine," they said. Even the fact that their daughter had been found in a hospital didn't shake them from their belief that this was just an elaborate prank she had pulled to get attention.

"What happened?" Nick asked. "Have you been here all this time?"

"I don't remember. I blacked out."

"You've been gone for two weeks."

"God, really?" Fish asked.

"Yeah."

"That's so weird."

"Fish . . ."

"What?"

"You sure you don't remember anything?"

"No. Wait. Yeah. Maybe. I remember being home sometimes. But then I would wake up and I would be somewhere else. I'm confused," she said. So she had been home. She had been the one stealing.

Fish began sobbing quietly. "I don't know what's happened. My mind is all blank. I'm trying to remember, but I can't, and I'm scared, Nick. What's happened to me?"

"Do you remember something about the back room? Something about a drink? It's red. It makes you feel . . . dreamy, sleepy," Nick said.

Fish's eyes lit up. "TAP . . . I remember that. I took that drink and then, I don't know . . . nothing."

The light went out of her eyes suddenly. Nick was concerned. The loud little stepsister he'd known was nowhere in that bed. Fish was a shell of her former self, almost as if she'd been drained—literally—of her entire personality. Sucked dry and spit out.

"Leave me alone, Nick," Fish said, turning her back to the wall.

The drug. The angel factor. He had to find out what was in it. Had to find out what it was really doing to kids.

welcome to
TAP.COM

 HOM
BROWSE
 EARCH
 NVITE
 ILM
MAIL
 LO
FAVORITES
ORUM
ROUP
VENT
IDE
MUSI
 CLASSIFIEDS

TAPPED IN....

Your news.
Your space.
Your funeral.
Put up
your stuff,
your videos,
your pics,
your photos,
your music.
Whateva
you gots for
us, we're
into it.

MEMBERSHIP IS FREE.
RESPECT IS NOT.

Member Login:

SCREEN NAME ☆

PASSWORD ☆

★
search TAP

TAPPED IN . . . The latest news from your world

1:45 PM **anon** writes:
ready for the biggest bash of the year???? **johnny**'s
back!! Hallelujah and praise the lord I've got tickets!
[Four comments] [Add a comment]

 COMMENTS

hopeless567: front row center.

king_geek3117: knew he'd be back!

platosrepublic5566: woohooooooooooooo

michelangelico8973: be there or be nowhere

Taj

IT WAS GOING TO BE THE BREAKTHROUGH
performance of a lifetime. Johnny Silver was back!
He'd been gone for a while, but he'd returned. He was
playing at the Hollywood Bowl, and Taj wouldn't miss
it for the world, even if she knew that that wasn't
Johnny up there with his guitar.

First she had to see Sutton. This had gone on long
enough. She didn't want any part of it anymore. And she
wanted to know where Johnny was. Wanted to make
sure he was really okay. Sutton had been kind enough to
send her several tickets and backstage passes.

There was the usual mad chaos backstage, and
Taj found him conferring with the stage director on
lighting issues.

"You're really going through with this," she said.

"Trust me, it's not how I planned it. I'd always wanted Johnny to come back himself, but he's forced me to find an alternative."

"Where is he, Sutton? I know you know. Where have you been hiding him?"

"Like I told you the other day, he's gone, Taj. He doesn't want anything to do with TAP anymore."

"So he just left? He's just poof—disappeared again?"

"I'm sure he'll turn up eventually. You know Johnny. He can take care of himself."

"Well, that's it for me. I'm getting out too," Taj said.

"Out? What do you mean, out? We haven't even begun yet," Sutton said. "And baby, I don't think you have much of a choice. You knew what was in TAP. You knew what was required. Plus, you knew what would happen if you really tried to get out."

He was right. She'd known all along. She had been the one to suggest they play Johnny's songs in the back room. She'd been the one who'd discovered Johnny, really. Who'd created the myth around him. And there was the angel factor. She'd been the one who had discovered how to make it, had suggested mixing it with Kool-Aid, giving it to kids in the back room at the parties.

"I don't care—I'm getting out. Or at the very least

I'm taking the songs. They're mine. I wrote them. I own them."

"Wrong again, Taj. Did you ever see that little disclaimer on the page? 'All contents on the TAP.com website are owned by TAP.com. Copyright TAP.com. No reproduction without permission from TAP.com.' Everything anyone puts up on the site is owned by TAP and by Werner Music. It's the same with any website— Amazon owns the reviews people write. Think about that next time you put something up on the Web."

Taj frowned. She hadn't figured that. "Fine. You own the songs. I can write others. But what I need to know is why?"

"Why?"

"Why did you let the gifting get out of hand?"

Sutton shrugged. "Why not? Why not see how far it could go? Besides, you know kids. They want more and more. They want stuff. They want friends. They want to be famous. They want to feel good. We provide all this. You and me, Taj.

"We've—if you'll forgive the pun—really tapped into something here. The gossip—that was your brilliant idea, about controlling behavior. The wish lists. Creating a desire. Keeping the cows dumb. Keeping everyone content. Distracting them. So that they don't see what's really out there."

"It was only supposed to be an experiment, a prank, nothing real," Taj said. "Nothing that would affect anything in the real world."

"It's very real, Taj. You know as well as I do."

"No."

"Suit yourself."

"You sent Nick that postcard, didn't you?" she said.

"Nick." He grimaced. "You should stay clear of that guy. He's never going to get it. He's a nonbeliever. Lots of bad energy."

"You wanted him to hate me," Taj said softly. "Maybe he already does. Did you know his friend is missing now too?"

"Oh, that kid. Yeah. We gave him a little scare. Told him to stop hacking into systems he shouldn't be concerned about. He's all right. I think you'll find him much chastened."

"Where are those missing kids, Sutton? What happened to them?"

"Most of them should be waking up now. It's a sad side effect of the drug. The angel factor isn't quite stable yet—it causes an allergic reaction in some. A pity."

"Where's Nick's sister?"

"She woke up. She's home. They're all home

Melissa de la Cruz

now. You see? Like I told you, there's been no harm. And hopefully she's learned her lesson. That's what happens when you get behind. When you try to leave."

"Fish was trying to get out?"

"She said she couldn't afford it anymore. But that's irrelevant. It's not part of the rules. Just because you can't score doesn't mean you can stop playing the game. Remember that, Taj. Remember what you promised."

"You're sick. And this cult you've created—"

"'Cult' is a strong word, Taj. You say cult; I say gathering of like minds."

"You're using the Web, and Johnny, as bait. He brought more people into TAP than anyone else. You used him to recruit kids."

"Oh, no—they came to us. But yes. So useful, your creation. Johnny Silver."

"Why?"

"Because every cult needs a messiah, Taj. And rock stars are perfect for it. I had thought Johnny was special. I had bought into it just as hard as anyone. It was a revelation when you told me the truth. Then I saw all the possibilities."

"You're crazy."

"Like I told you at the hotel, I had thought

Johnny would be the one to take TAP to the next level, but he was only a vessel, able to receive and send, but not able to create. But you, Taj . . ."

"Me?"

"Those songs you wrote. Those ideas you had. You're a natural. Don't deny it. And besides, it's too late now."

"What's it all about, Sutton?" Taj sighed. He was right. It was too late. She'd signed her name in blood. She'd made the pact. They all had.

"The usual story." Sutton shrugged. "Sex, drugs, rock and roll. Isn't that what every teen wants? And fame. Yes. Fame is a new thing now. Did you know that sixty percent of America's teenagers believe they will become famous? For no reason at all. Not talent, certainly. But they believe it. And they put up their TAP pages and they wait for the call to come in. For almost all of them, the call will never come, but in the meantime, there's TAP."

"Five minutes, Mr. Silver," a stagehand called.

"Now, if you'll excuse me, I need to prepare my client for his show. And Taj? I trust we'll see you at the next meeting?"

Taj nodded her head. "Yes."

Johnny

HE WALKED OUT OF THE IN-N-OUT BURGER, WIPING his hands on his pants. He was still shaking, and his mind was a muddle. The kid he'd met in there had told him he was supposed to be onstage at the Hollywood Bowl at that moment. That didn't make any sense. But then nothing seemed to make sense anymore. Not since the night of the light.

What he'd told the kid was the truth. All he remembered was a blinding white light, and then he'd woken up in the desert, alone. For a long time he'd just been wandering by himself, hungry.

Then a car had arrived to pick him up. Out of nowhere, as if it had known where to find him.

There was a guy in the car who looked familiar. The guy said his name was Sutton, and he was a friend. The guy took him back to a hotel; it was a nice one in Palm Springs. He remembered the name of the town because he'd been there as a kid.

They'd stayed there for a while, and then the guy took him to another hotel. The guy kept asking him if he thought he could play, but when he picked up a guitar, he looked at it and didn't remember anything. Too bad, said the guy—Sutton—remember—his name was Sutton.

It was so hard to remember things now. Like his name. Sutton had said that if anyone asked, his name was Johnny. Johnny was a nice name, so he'd liked that.

That's what the kid called him. Aren't you Johnny Silver? The boy had asked. And for the first time, it resonated. Johnny Silver. He had been Johnny Silver. But he didn't know who he was anymore. Not after the light.

Sutton had taken him to another nice hotel, high up in the hills, with a great view. It looked familiar. And the other day he was asleep in his bed and he heard a girl's voice. It, too, had sounded familiar. It sounded like home.

The girl . . . he had to find the girl. She would know. She would know how to help him. She knew everything. She always did. That much he remembered.

Melissa de la Cruz

So today, he decided he wanted to walk outside, and he found himself in front of the In-N-Out Burger.

He'd walked in and ordered the number one. That he remembered. He'd always gotten the number one before.

He took a deep breath. He was still confused and disoriented, and sad. He felt the tears falling freely on his cheeks. He had no idea why he was crying. Something about remembering that night had made him sad. But no matter. He liked being outside. Sutton kept him inside all the time. Wouldn't let him do anything but order room service.

The light changed, and Johnny crossed the street. He didn't know where he was going, didn't know where he was from. But all he knew was he had to find her. He had to find the girl who had given him his name.

Nick

HE SPENT THE EVENING DRIVING AROUND, TRYING TO get in touch with her, but she never picked up her phone. Finally he decided he would do what she had done. He would wait for her in front of her house.

"Hey," she said, not looking the least bit surprised to find him sitting on her porch at one in the morning.

"I've seen Johnny," he said.

"You mean at the Bowl."

"No, I mean at the In-N-Out. Just now. He looked like he was on something. He was barely coherent."

"Interesting." So Sutton hadn't lied—Johnny had left on his own.

"That's it? You think it's interesting?"

"What do you want, Nick?" she asked.

Neither of them was sure just what had happened

between them, but the easy camaraderie between them had changed—shifted.

"What are they going to do with that kid up onstage at the Bowl? The pretender. Is he going to disappear too? Listen, I don't know what you are doing, but I know you need to keep away from Sutton. He's dangerous," Nick said finally.

"Nick."

"We need to find out more about TAP. That drink they give the kids—it's dangerous. It's fucked up Fish. She's not the same person. We need to stop them. Will you help me?"

"No," Taj said quietly.

Nick turned to her. "What do you mean, no?"

In answer, she showed him the inside of her wrist. Something that wasn't there before. A tattoo. The angel wings. *One million years of allegiance*. It was a joke, she'd said. She'd dismissed it as nothing. But perhaps that was a lie too. She was one of them. She'd been Tapped.

"What does this mean?" he asked, holding her wrist up to the light and not quite believing what he was seeing.

She drew him closer, put her light hand on his cheek. He put a hand on top of hers.

She lifted up her chin and he leaned down. She

kissed him. A long, passionate kiss. A kiss like the one they'd shared at the station. They kissed, and for Nick it was like time had stopped. He pulled her into his arms. Things were going to be okay. This was okay. This was what he had been waiting for.

Then she drew back. She looked at him sorrowfully.

"This is good-bye, Nick."

"What?"

"We can't see each other anymore."

"Because of Johnny? Because you're still in love with Johnny?" he asked, his voice tight.

"No. It has nothing to do with Johnny," she said, but she wouldn't meet his eyes.

"But why then?"

"TAP is about loving everyone, not just one person. I'm sorry, Nick," she said, as if she were reading from a script. Her eyes were blank and remote.

Then she walked into the house and locked the door.

This time, Nick could actually feel his heart breaking. And he realized that he'd been wrong. You could fall in love at seventeen. Desperately in love. No matter what she had done before, or why she was involved in the shadowy world of TAP, she was in something deep and scary and he needed to get her out. He needed to rescue her. He was going to find a

Melissa de la Cruz

way. If it was the last thing he did in his life, he swore he would do it.

Nick Huntington walked down the steps, took one last look back at Taj's house, got in his car, and drove back to the Westside.

welcome to
TAP.COM

HOME

BROWSE

SEARCH

INVITE

FILM

MAN

BLOG

FAVORITES
GROUP
GROUP
EVENT
IDEO
MUSIC
CLASSIFIEDS

TAPPED IN....

Your news.
Your space.
Your funeral.
Put up
your stuff,
your videos,
your pics,
your photos,
your music.
Whateva
you gots for
us, we're
into it.

**MEMBERSHIP IS FREE.
RESPECT IS NOT.**

Member Login:

SCREEN NAME☆

PASSWORD☆

search TAP

NickH3112
NickH3112 is in your
TAP network!
Tapped in: 2006
Male
17 years old
Single/Straight
Bel-Air
About me:
Varsity Soccer Captain,
Varsity Crew, Varsity
Tennis, BHCC, NHS

View my wish lists:
None

"never give up"

NickH3112's blog

Last Login: 7:55 PM
NickH3112 has 32 TAP friends.
View my pics/videos

COMMENTS

TajMahal22: hey nick, don't worry about me. remember,
you have to find your own way. i hope to see you when
you do. Peace & love. T.

[Click to Search for Friends] [Hot New People] [TAPPED IN Archives]

| HOME | BROWSE | SEARCH | INVITE | FILM | MAIL | BLOG |
| FAVORITES | FORUM | GROUPS | EVENTS | VIDEO | MUSIC | CLASSIFIEDS |

TAPPED IN....

Your news.
Your space.
Your funeral.
Put up
your stuff,
your videos,
your pics,
your photos,
your music.
Whateva
you gots for
us, we're
into it.

MEMBERSHIP IS FREE.
RESPECT IS NOT.

Member Login:

SCREEN NAME☆

PASSWORD☆

search TAP

TajMahal22
TajMahal22 is in your
TAP network!
Tapped in: 2005

Female
99 years old
Single/Straight
Hollywood
About me:
TAP-Org, Skaters
rule, ArtForum,
AltMusic, The
MiSTakes

View my wish lists:
* Amazon
* Skatergear.com
[See 83 more]

"is this me? love and loyalty"

TajMahal22's blog
Last Login: 4:11 AM
TajMahal22 has 52,398 TAP
friends
View my pics/videos

COMMENTS

NickH3112: Don't do this, Taj. I know you. Don't do
this.

SuttonW01: Today is the first day of the rest of your
life.

HOM BROWSE SEARCH NVIT ILM MAI BLOG
FAVORITES ORUM ROUP VENT IDE MUSI CLASSIFIEDS

TAPPED IN....

Your news.
Your space.
Your funeral.
Put up
your stuff,
your videos,
your pics,
your photos,
your music.
Whateva
you gots for
us, we're
into it.

**MEMBERSHIP IS FREE.
RESPECT IS NOT.**

JohnnyS11
**JohnnyS11 is in your TAP
network!**
Tapped in: 2004
Male
18 years old
Single/Straight
Los Angeles

View my wish lists:
[No new wish list items]

"did they get you to trade your
heroes for ghosts?"

**JohnnyS11's blog
Download Songs:**
[Secret Chord]
[Daze]
[Grand Illusion]
[Alternate Reality]
[View 10 more]
Last Login: 5:55 AM
**JohnnyS11 has 1,133,555
TAP friends**
View my pics/videos

COMMENTS

SuttonW01: Fantastie show the other night, my friend.
Bravo!

Acknowledgments

THANK YOU TO EVERYONE IN MY S&S FAMILY:
Emily Meehan, Elizabeth Law, Rick Richter, Courtney Bongiolatti, Michelle Montague, Jen Bergstrom, Bethany Buck, Paul Crichton, and Karen Frangipane. Thank you for believing in me, for supporting my work, and for all the wonderful book parties!

Thank you to everyone at ICM, especially Richard Abate and Josie Freedman.

Big ups to JDK (Jennie Kim), who helped with all the skateboarding research. Any and all mistakes in the skater text or lingo are my own.

Many thanks to my cousin Sigmund Torre, magna-artist extraordinaire, for the fabulous character portraits.

Thanks and love to my DLC family: Pop, Mom,

Chit, Aina, Steve, Nico, and Joe. And my Johnston family: Dad J., Mom J., John, Anji, Alex, Tim, Rob, Jenn, Val, and Lily.

Thanks and love to all my friends in L.A. and New York. (And my friends all over the world—in Kiev and Buenos Aires, especially!)

Thanks mostly to my husband, Mike, for dreaming up the TAP when I told him I was writing a book about cults in L.A.

Thanks to baby Mattie, who was with me every step of the way

Melissa de la Cruz